KORGi

CREATED BY

ANN & CHRISTIAN SLADE

top
Shelf
PRODUCTIONS

CHRISTIAN SLADE

KORGI

BOOK 1

TOP SHELF PRODUCTIONS

ATLANTA / PORTLAND

KORGI (BOOK 1): SPROUTING WINGS! © & TM 2007 CHRISTIAN SLADE.

PUBLISHED BY
TOP SHELF PRODUCTIONS
PO Box 1282
Marietta, GA 30061-1282
USA

PUBLISHERS:
CHRIS STAROS & BRETT WARNOCK

Visit our online catalog at
www.topshelfcomix.com.

Second Printing. June 2009. Printed in Canada.

Thanks to Chris, Brett
and the Top Shelf family

Fellow artist friends
Brad, J Pat, Ken, Neil, Mike, and Ray

Janice, Deb, Kandee, Art & Pat, Thyra
and all the corgi people who have
supported my work over the years

Special thanks to my family,
Mom, Dad, Maggie, David & Ann

Extra special thanks to
Queenie, Will, Wanda, Penny, Leo
and all the welsh corgis in the world

Thank you
for helping me find Korgi!

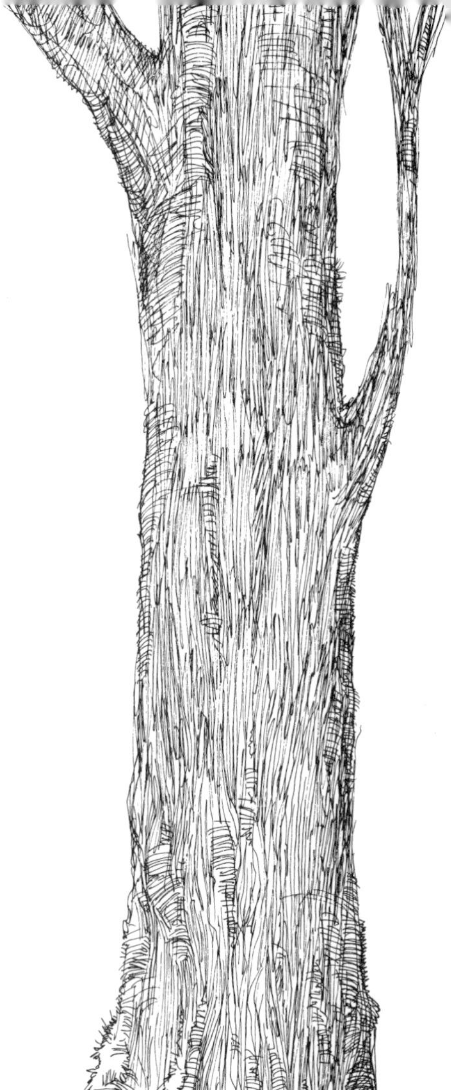

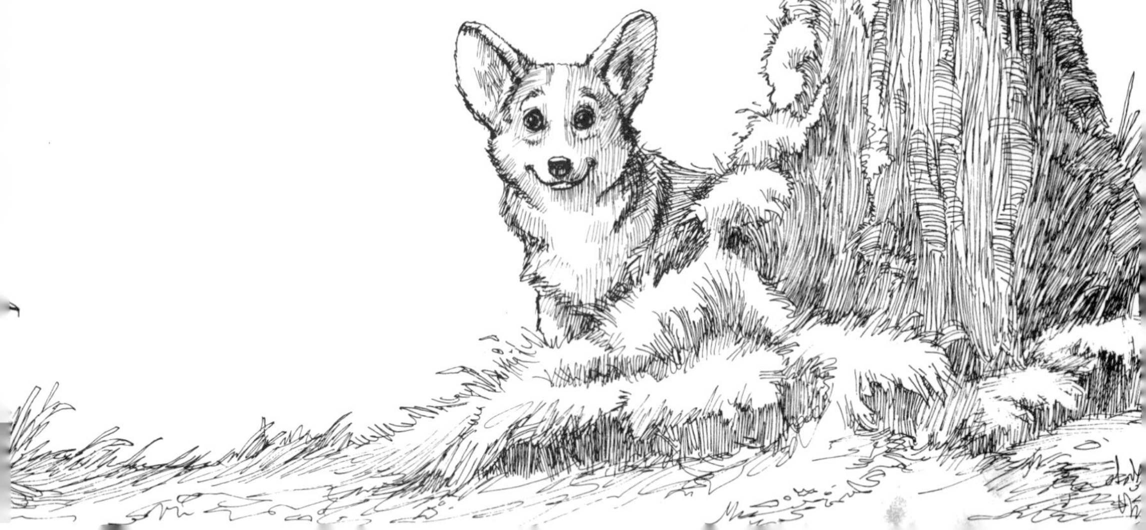

1

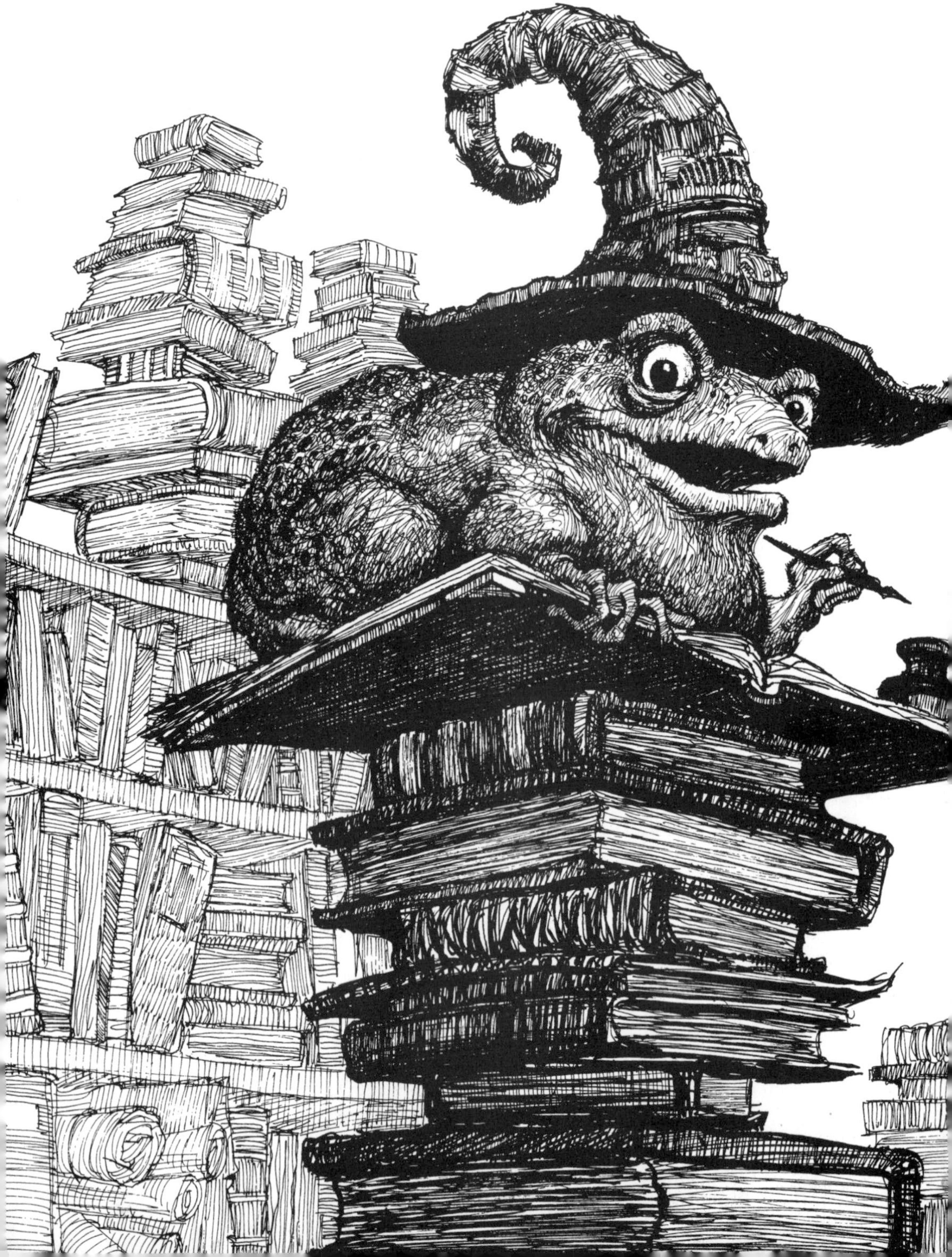

HELLO THERE! I've been waiting for you. I knew you would find your way here. Korgis, as you are about to discover, have a magical way about them. Travelers have always been drawn to these fox-like creatures. To be near them, is to feel more alive and happy than one has ever known. This is the great gift of the Korgi. They make the world around them more beautiful.

I know this because it is my purpose to know. I am Wart, the scrollkeeper of Korgi Hollow, the village with the last known Korgis left in this land.

Life was difficult before the Korgis came to live with us. We were a weak gathering of woodfolk called Mollies, with very little strength and smarts.

Since the Korgis have arrived, we are a happier and stronger community working together. The Korgis are now part of our family.

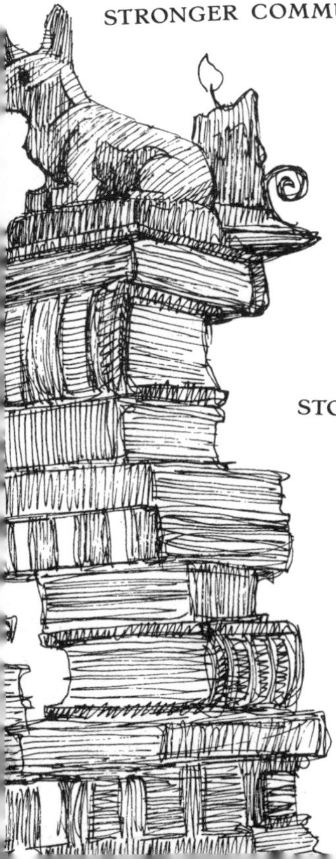

However, we must be careful. Evil monsters lurk in the surrounding woods, mountains and lakes. We cannot let any harm come to these special animals.

And now dear Reader, you will get to experience Korgis for yourself. This is the story of the young Mollie, Ivy, and her curious Korgi cub, Sprout, in a tale called,

"SPROUTING WINGS!"

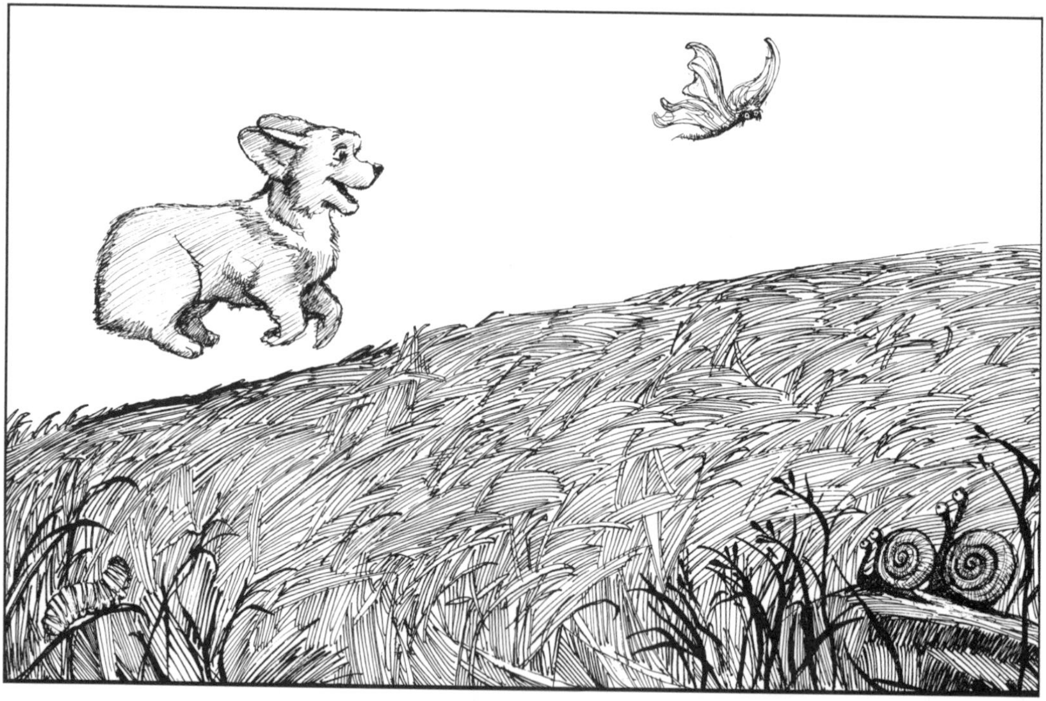

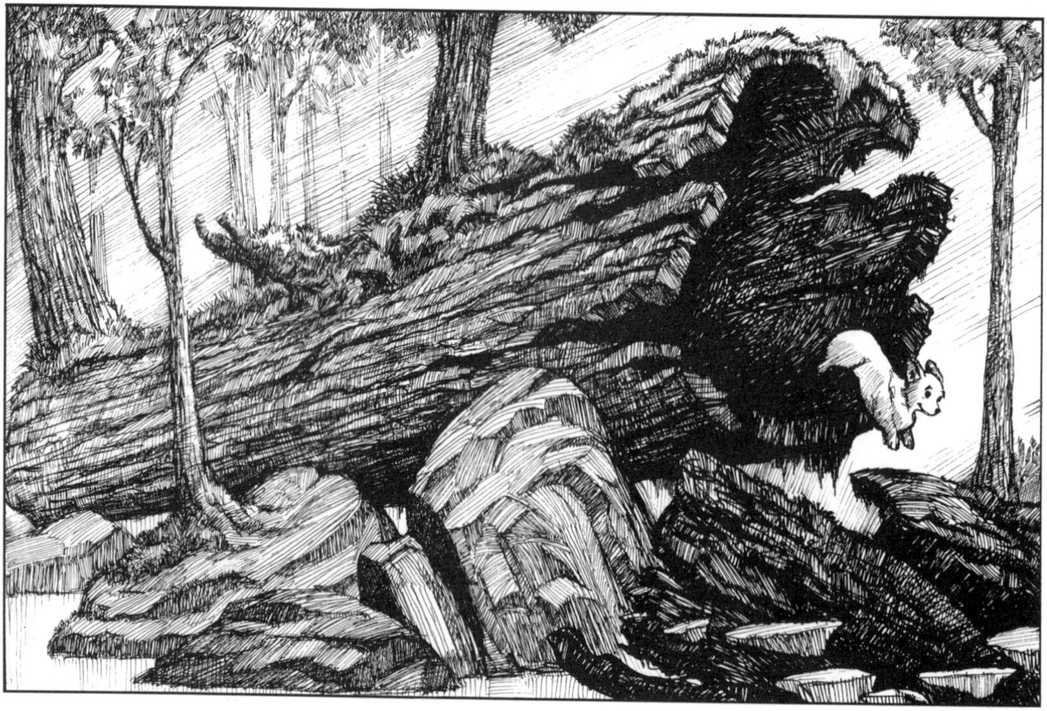

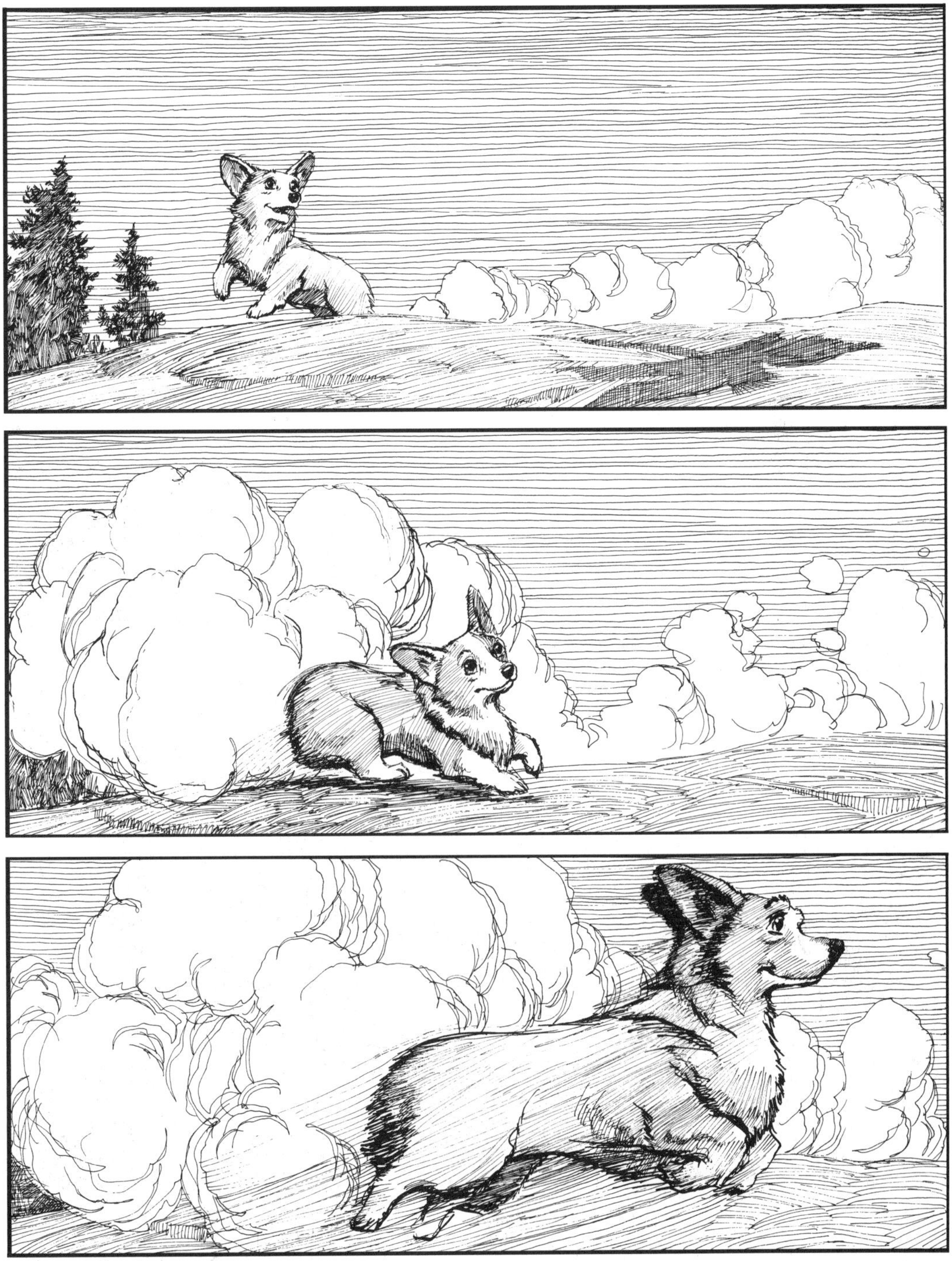

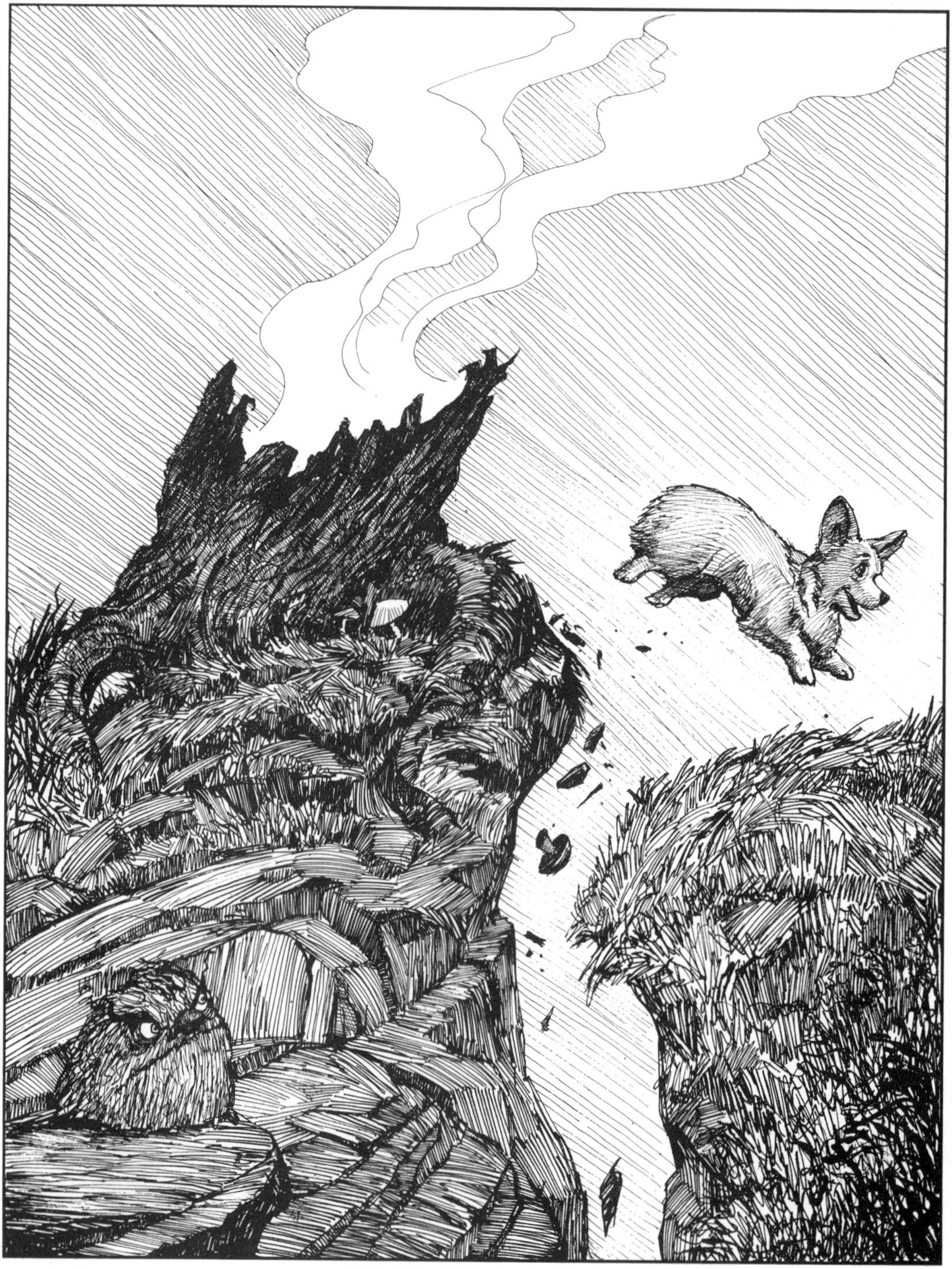

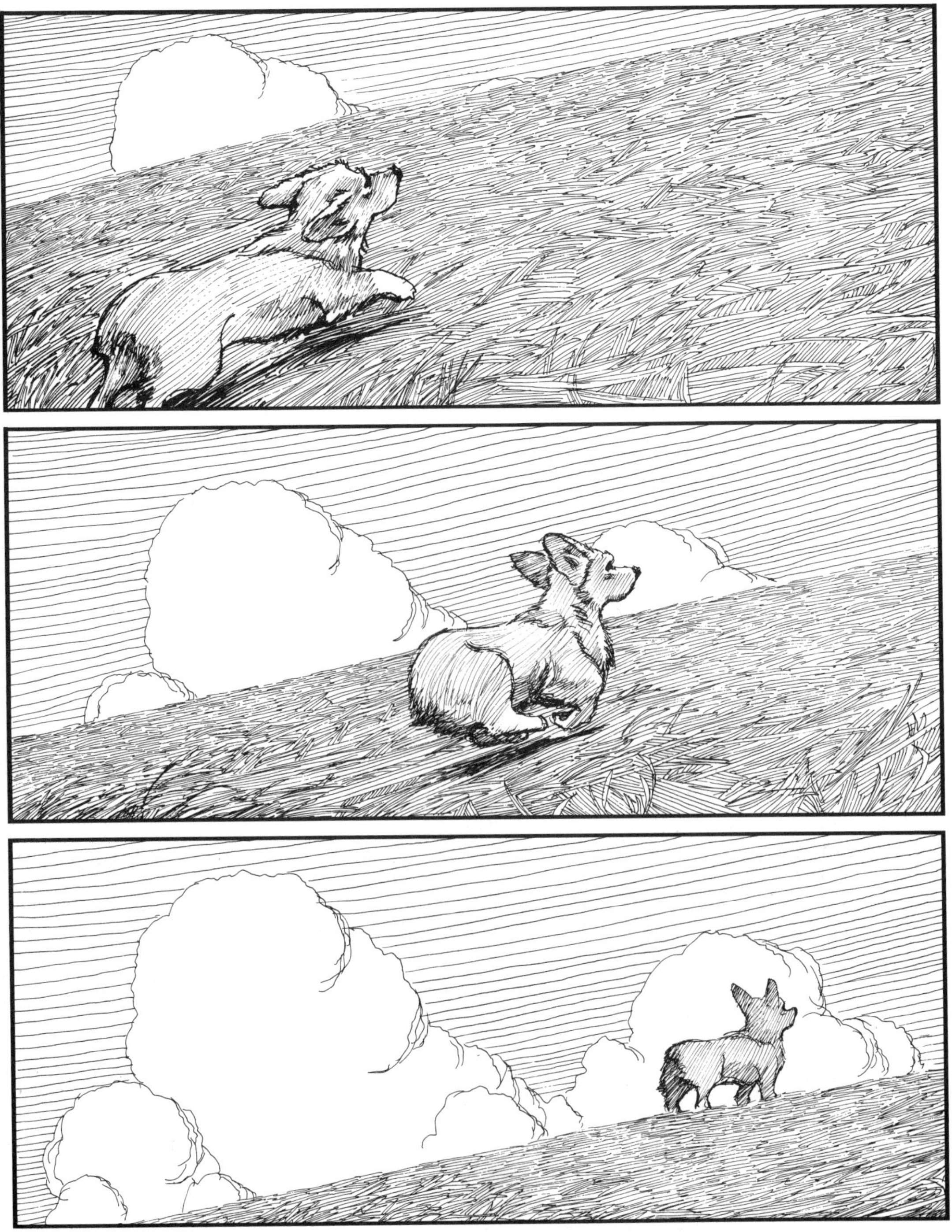

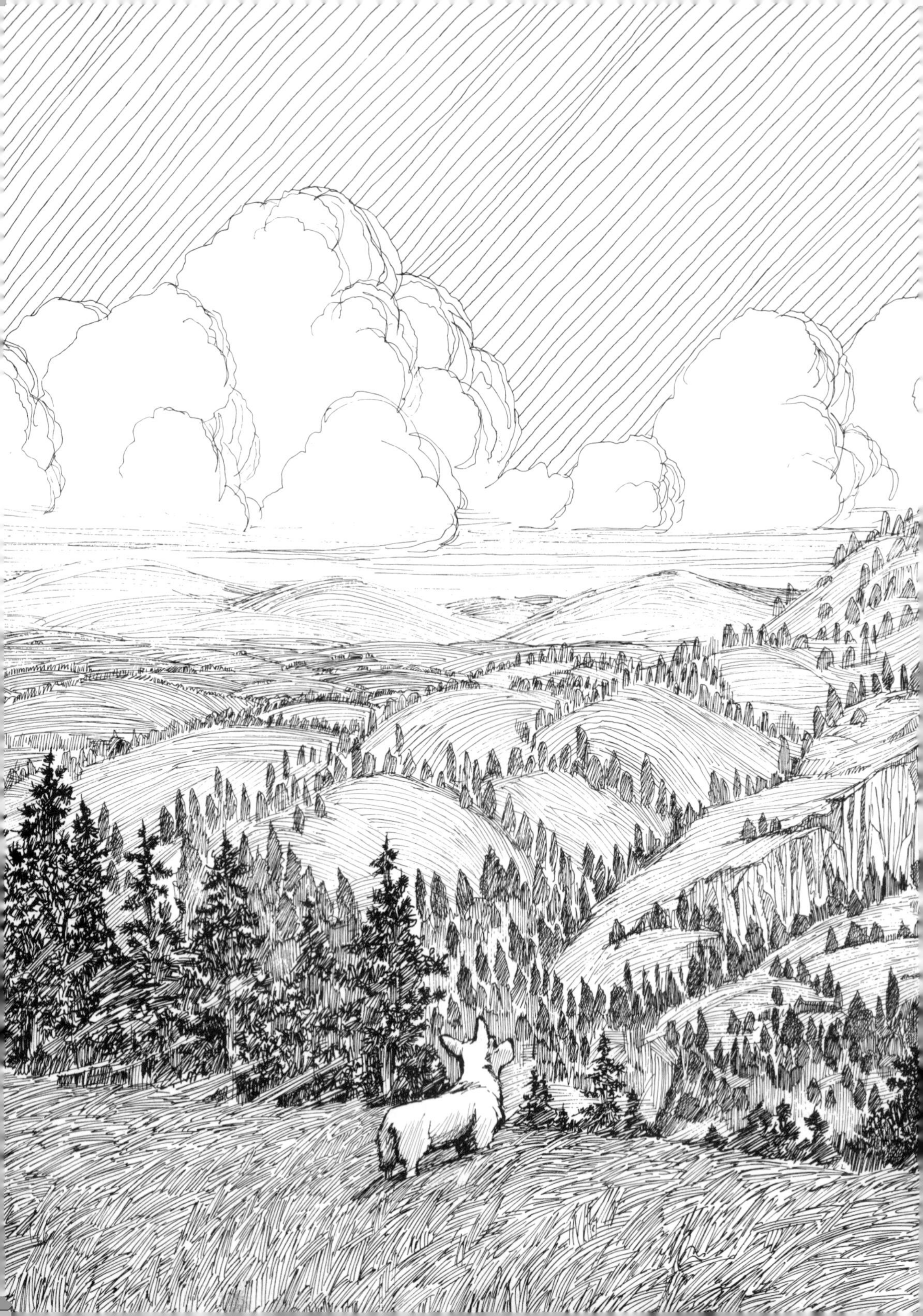

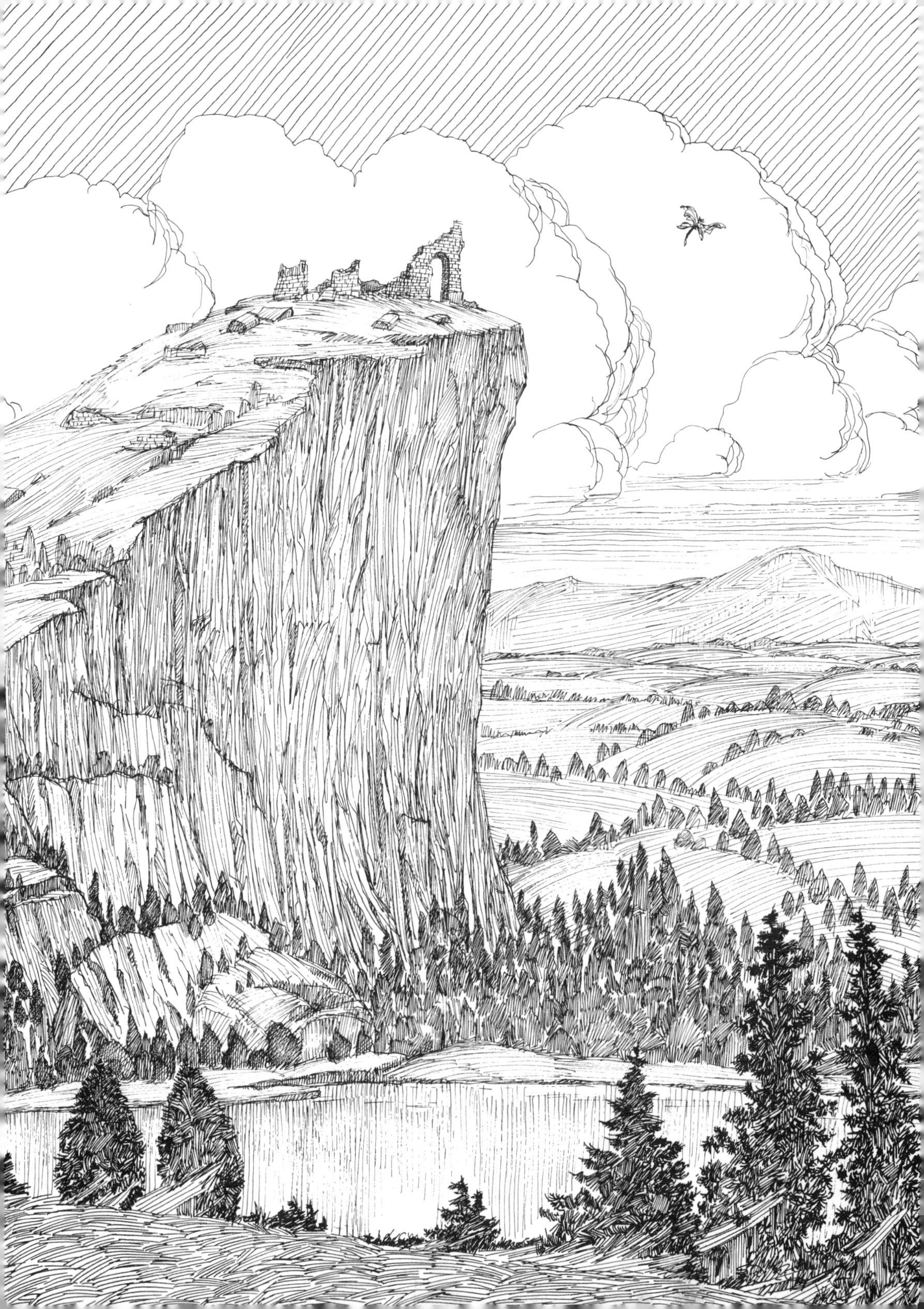

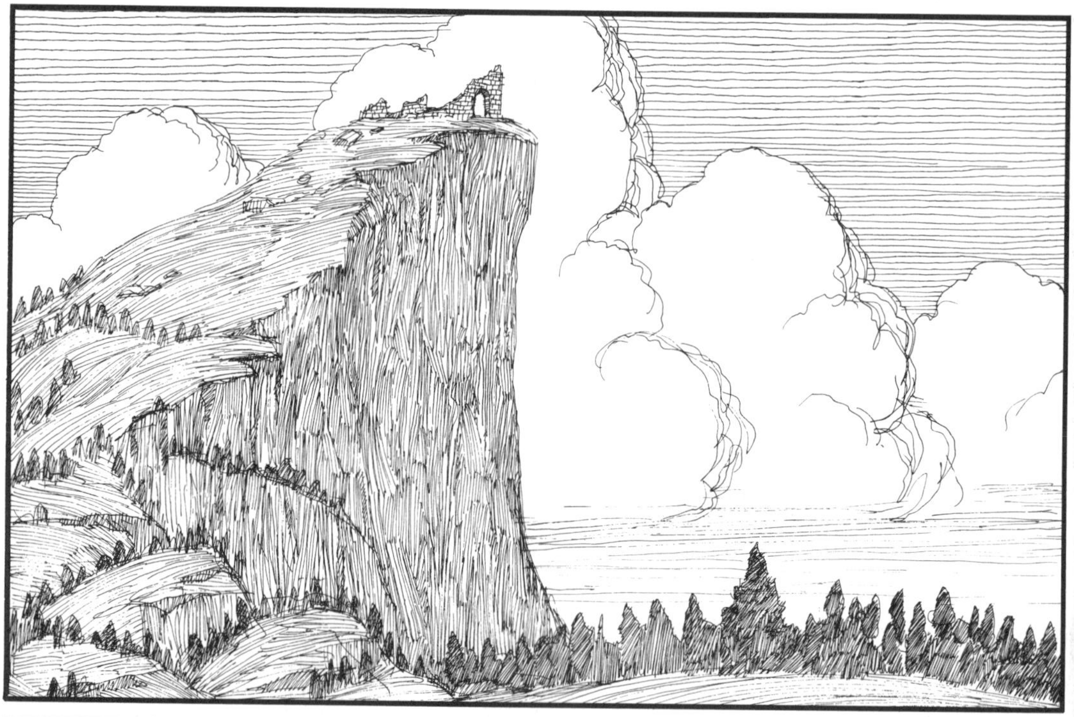

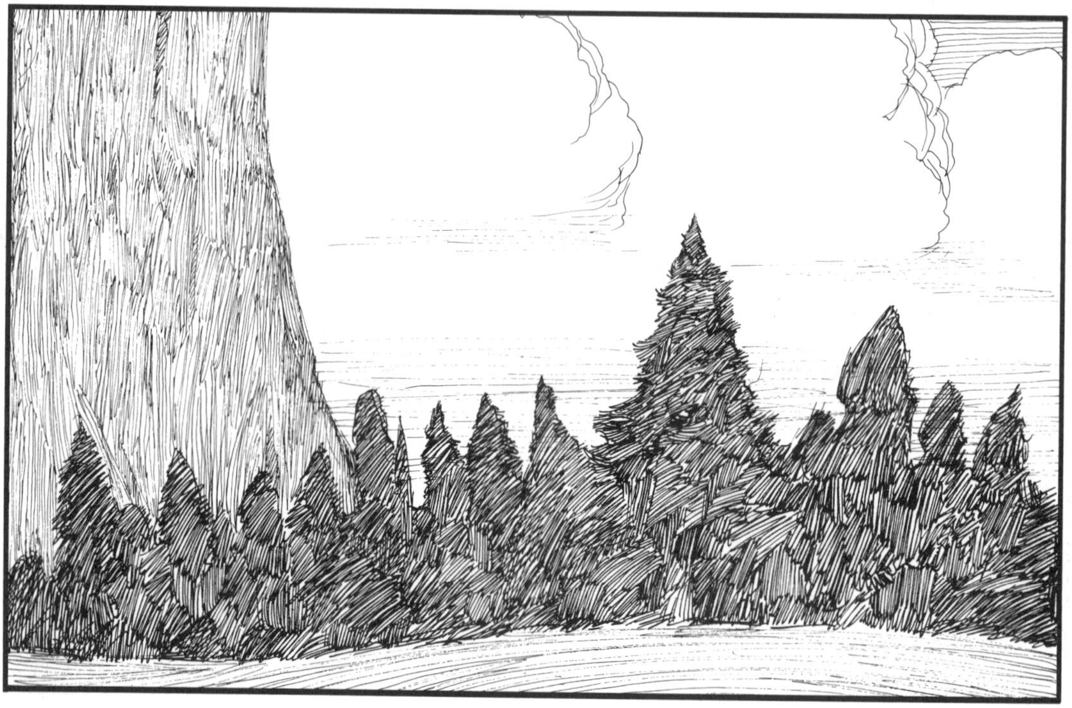

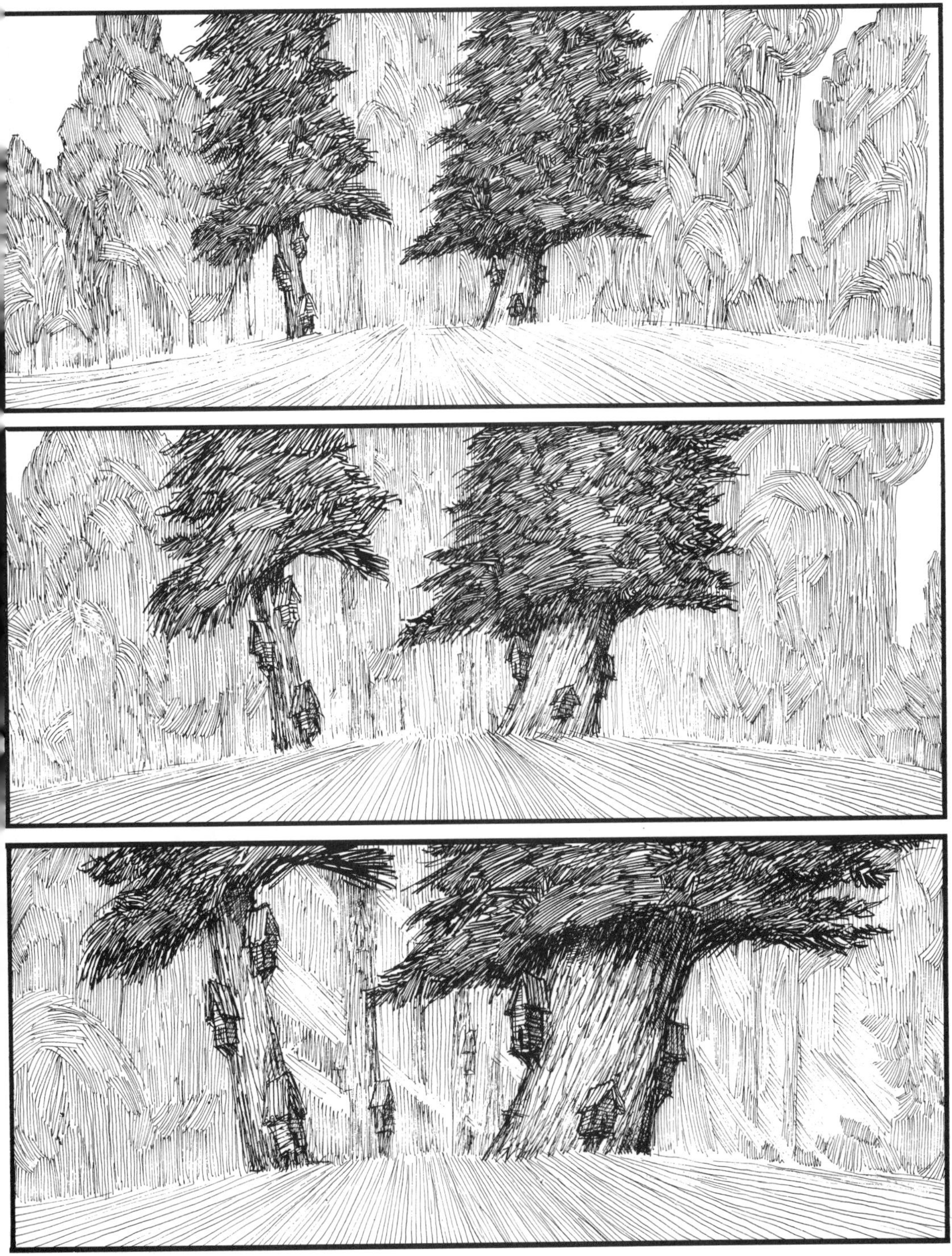

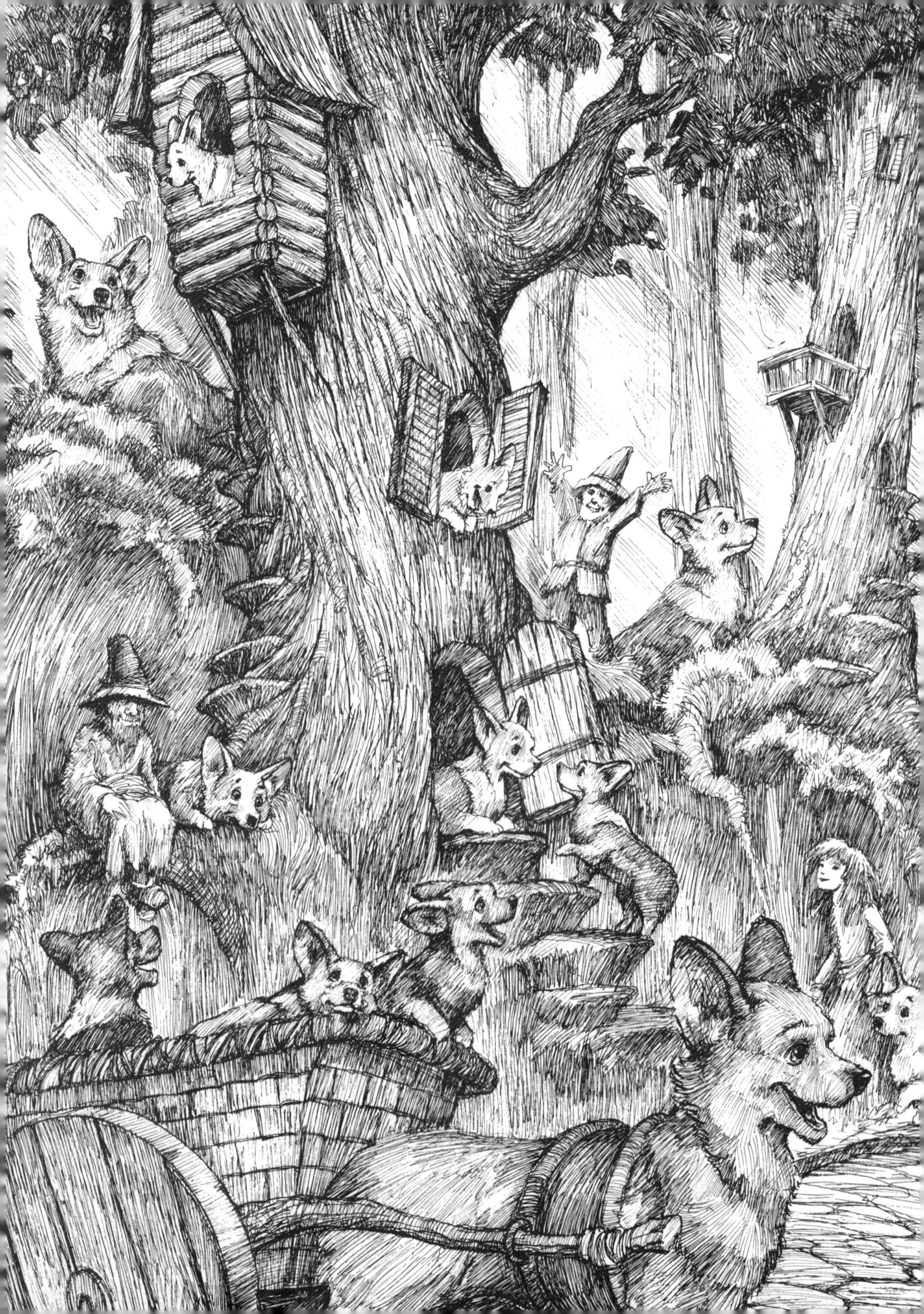

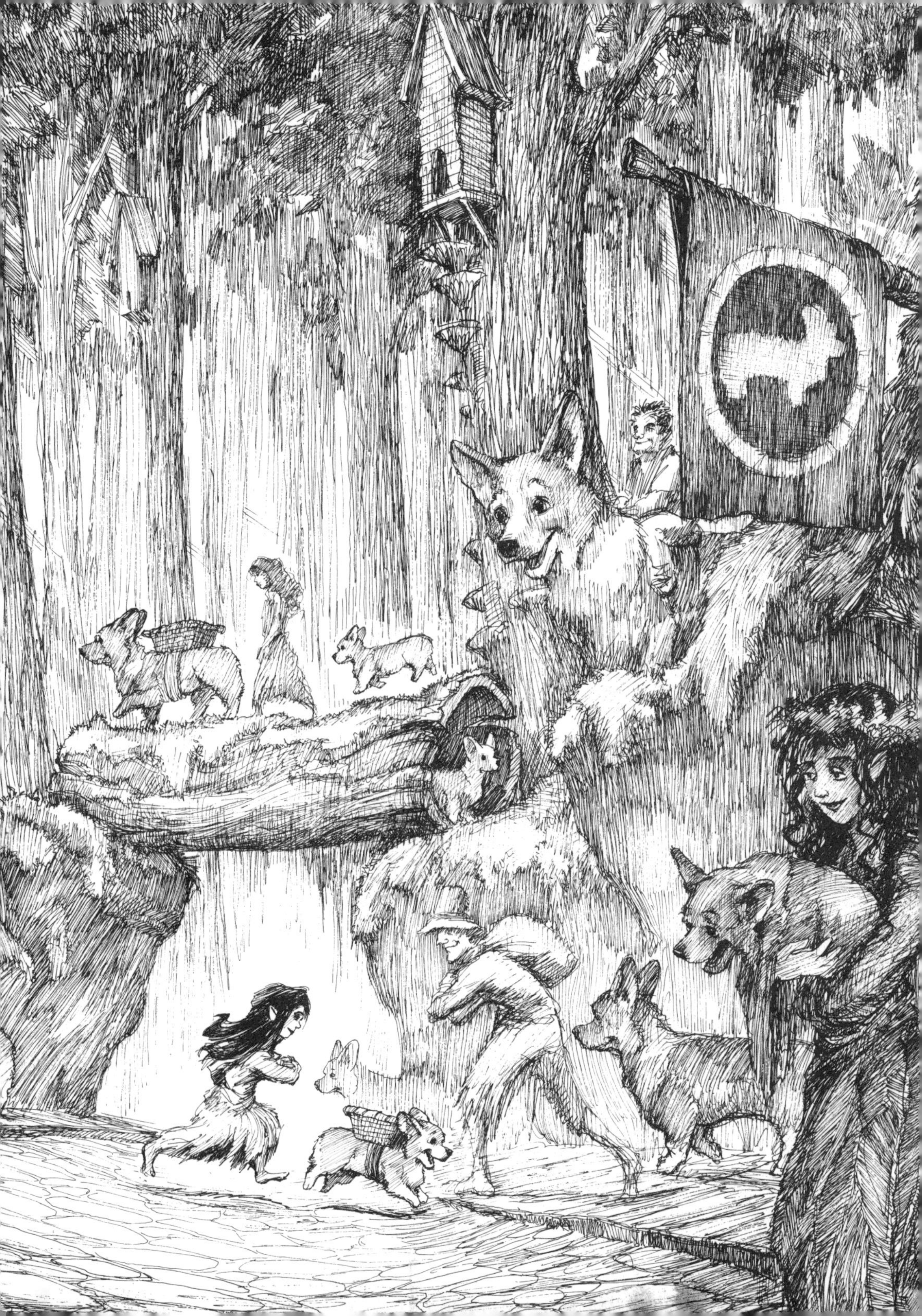

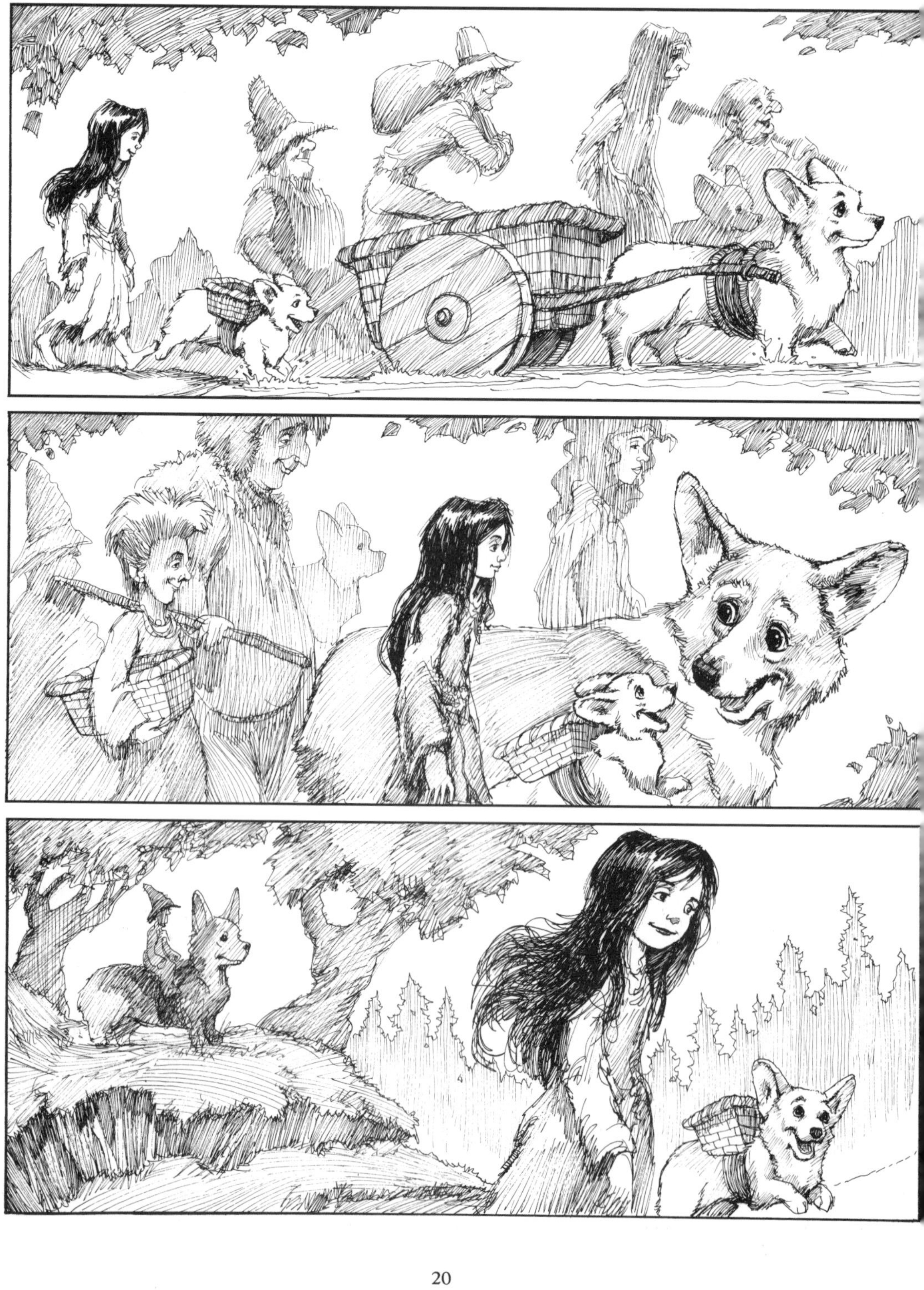

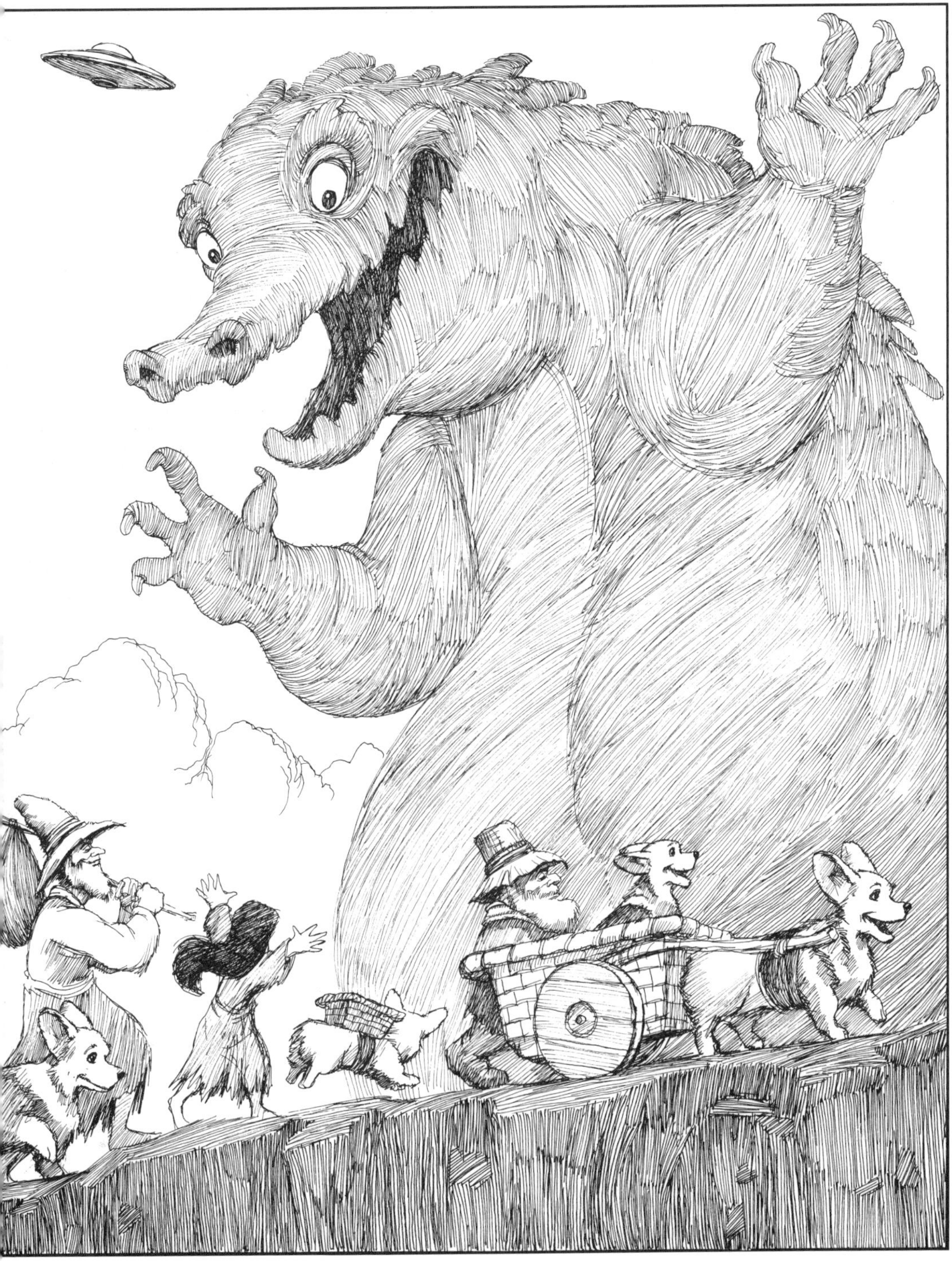

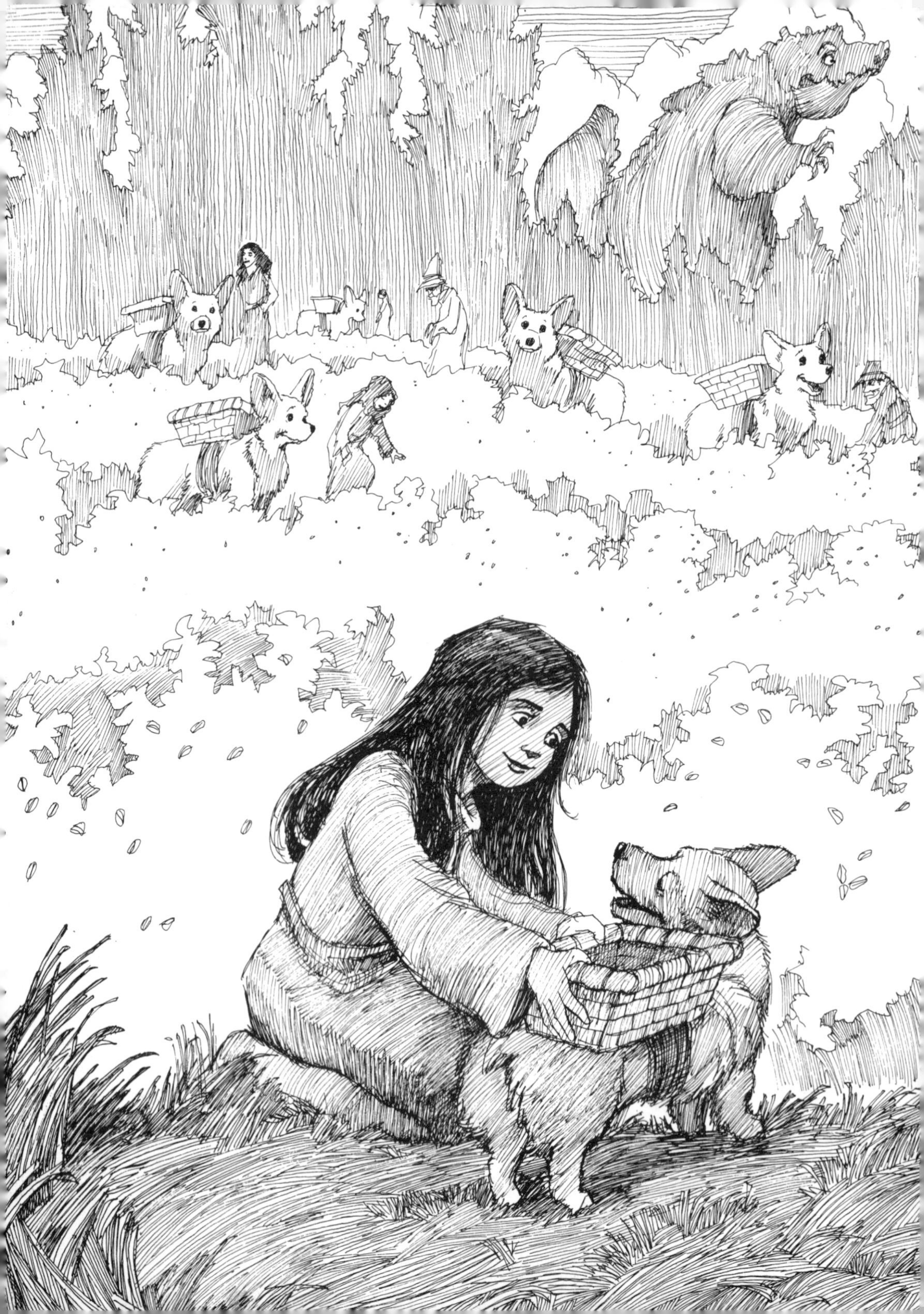

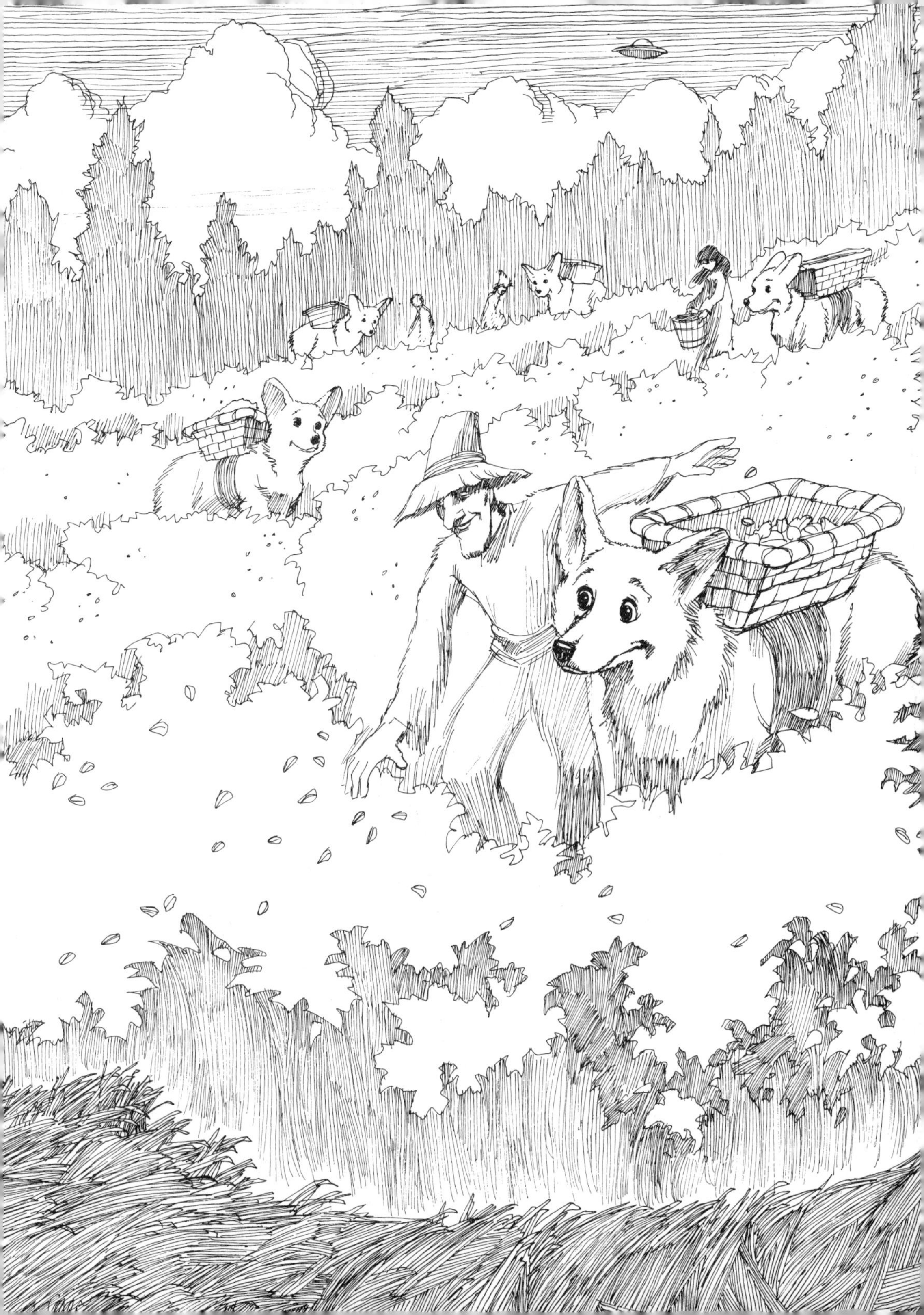

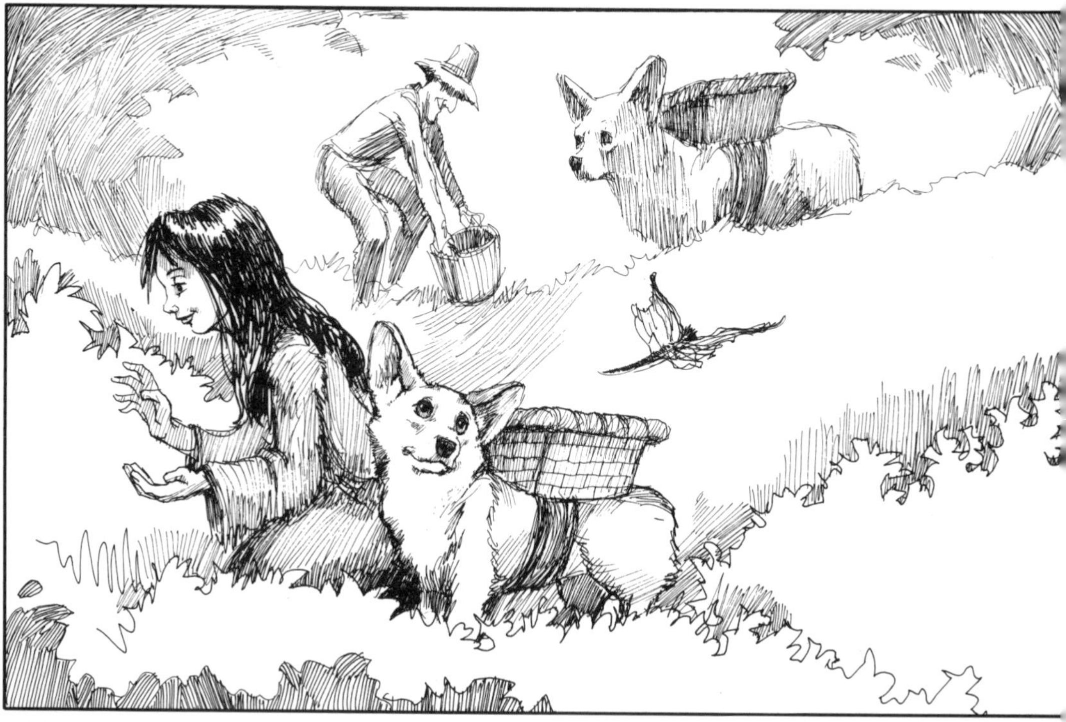

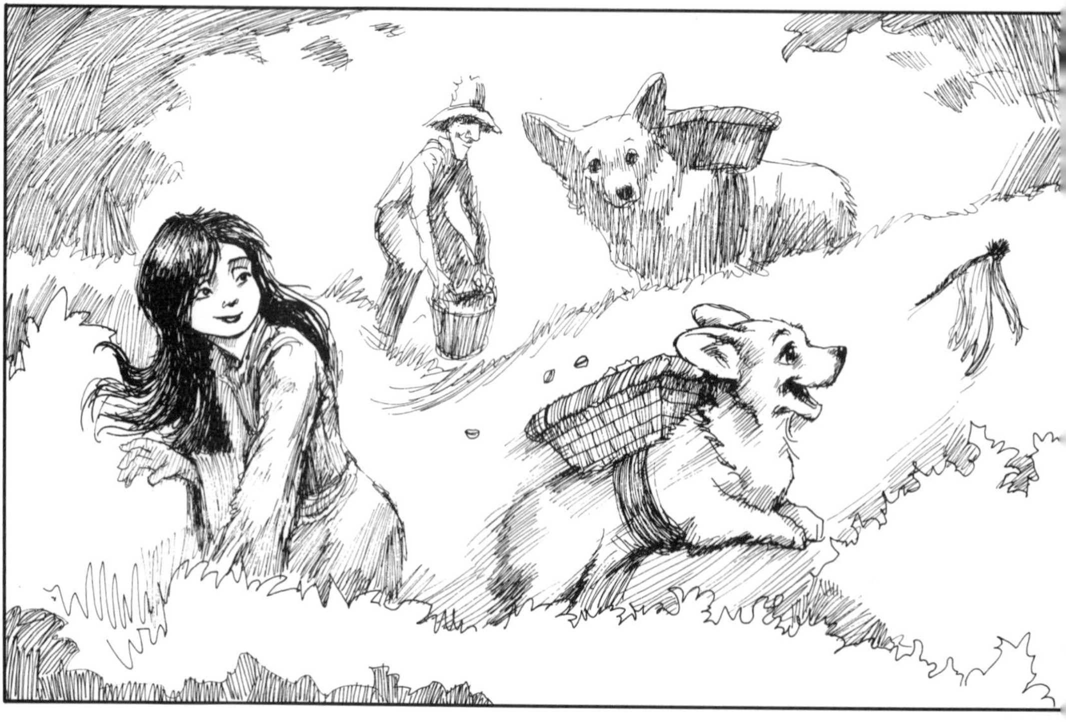

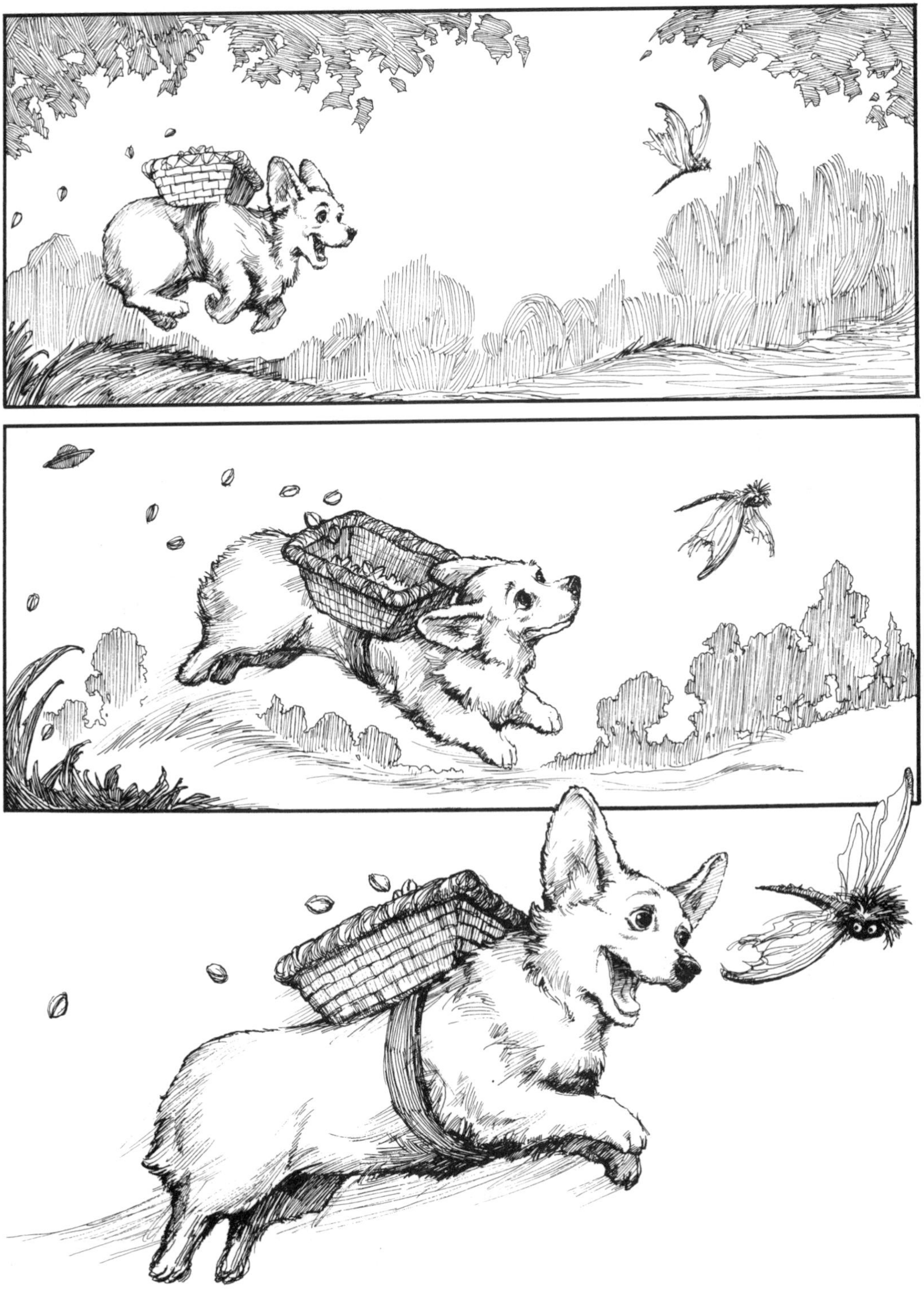

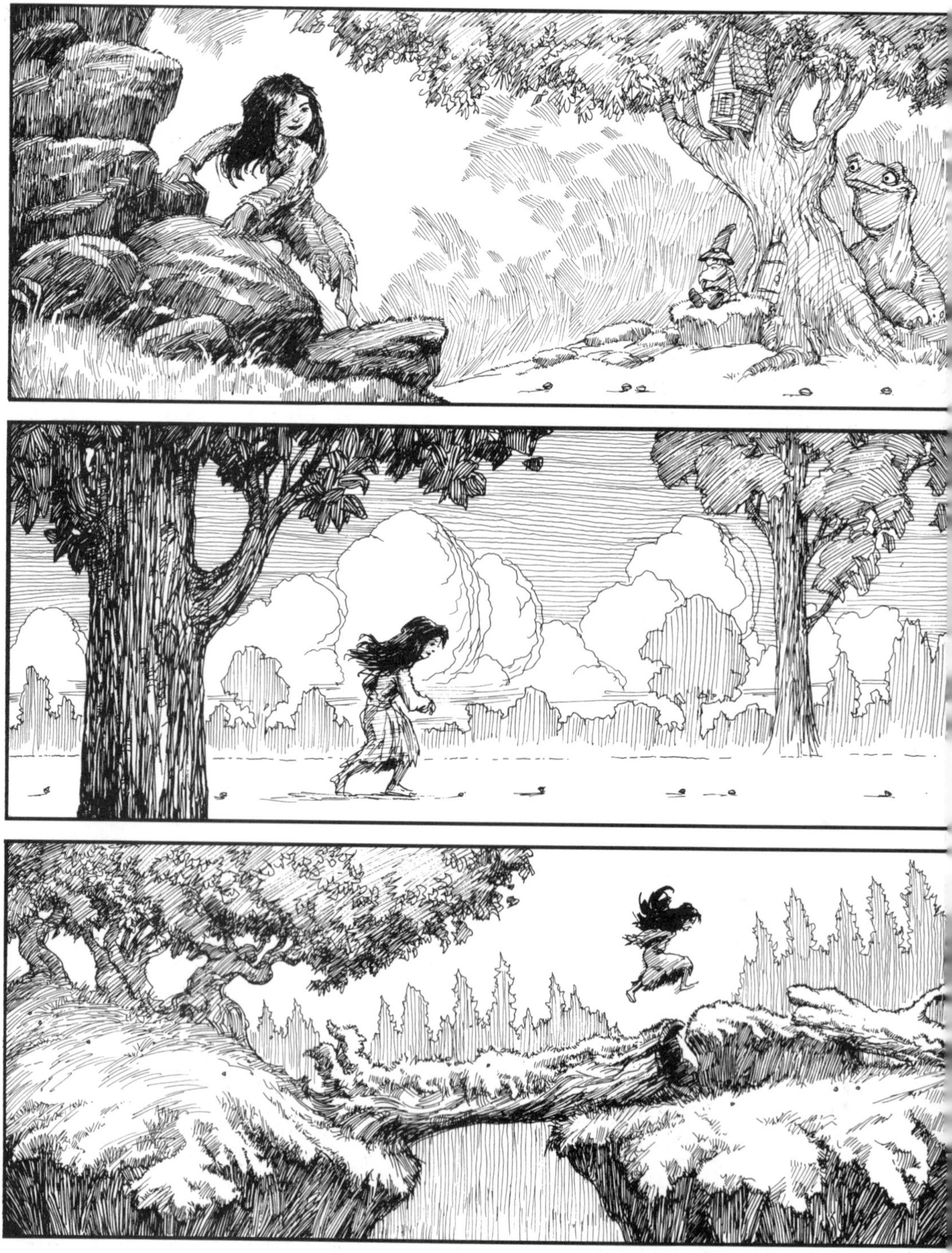

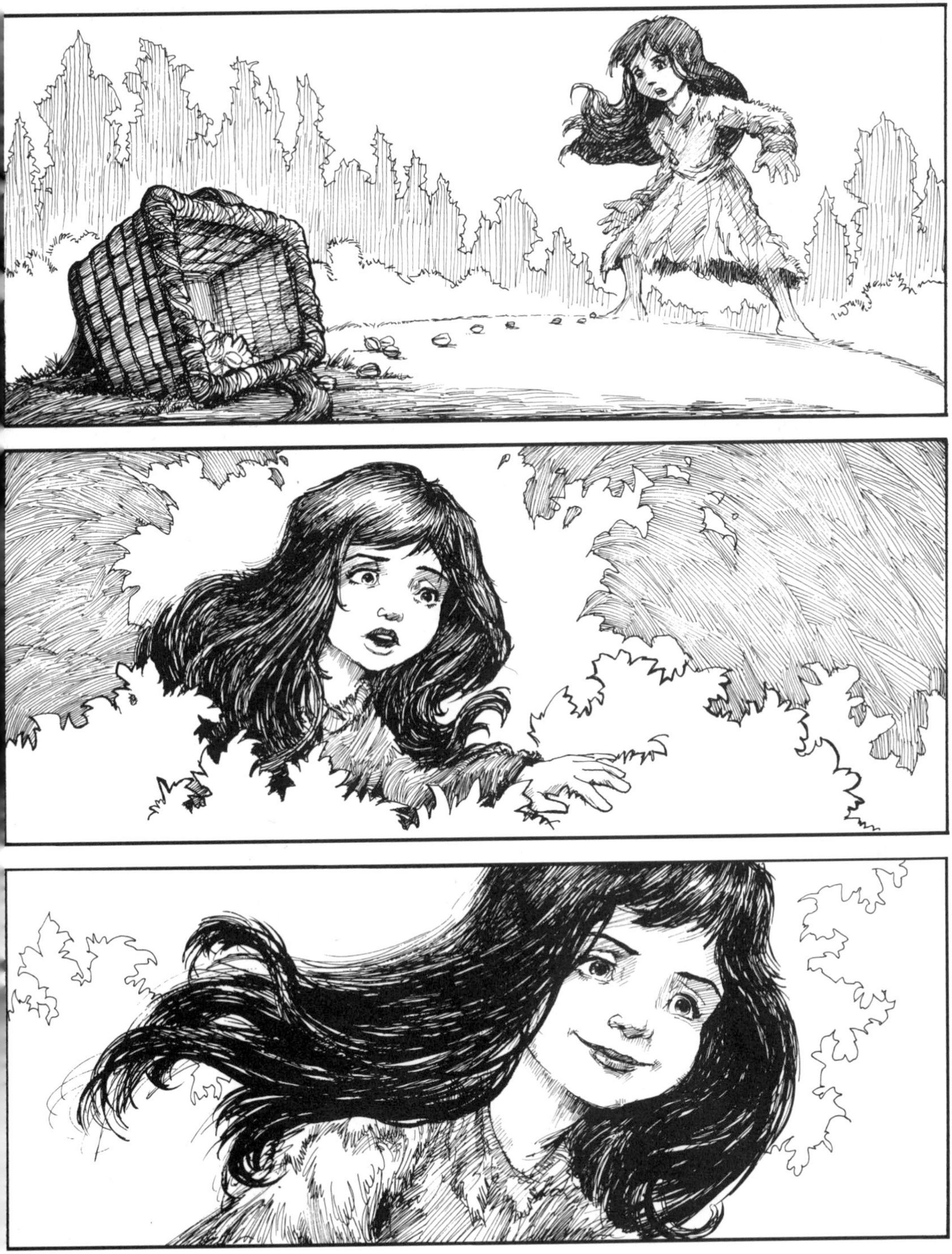

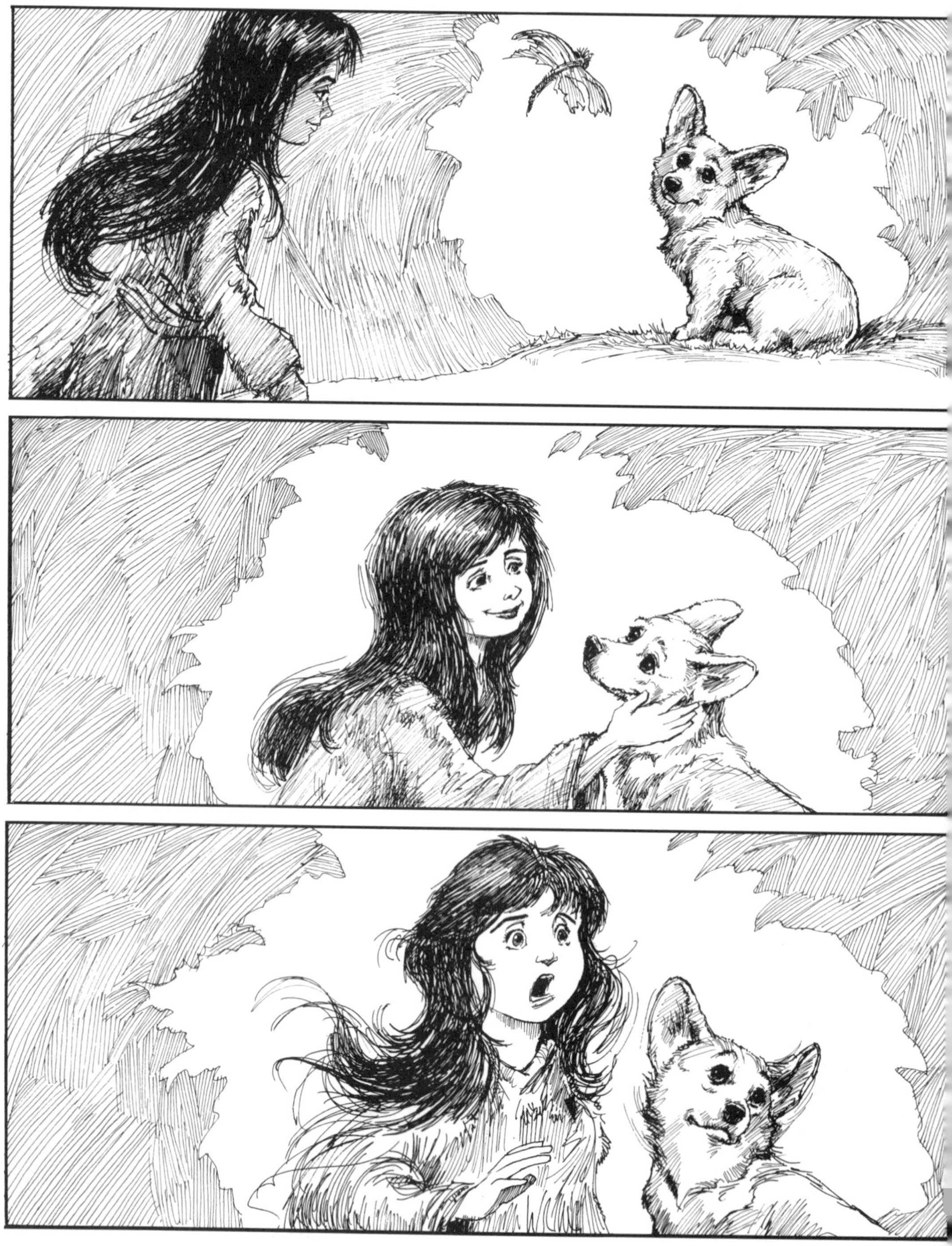

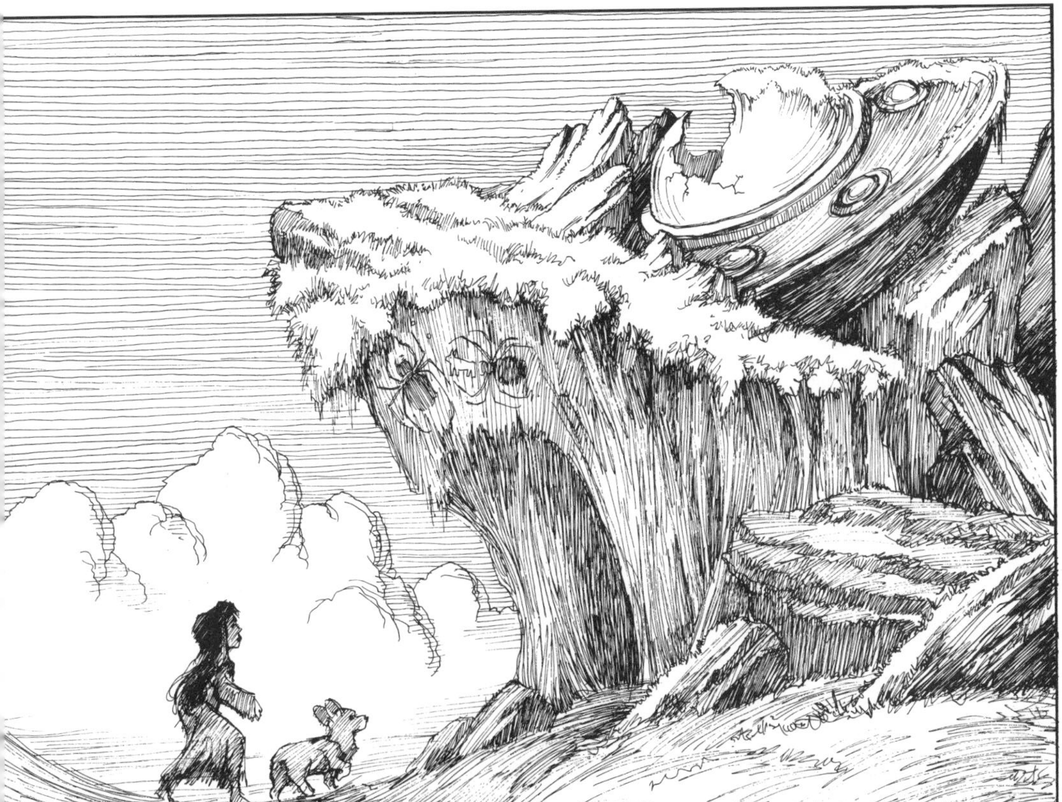

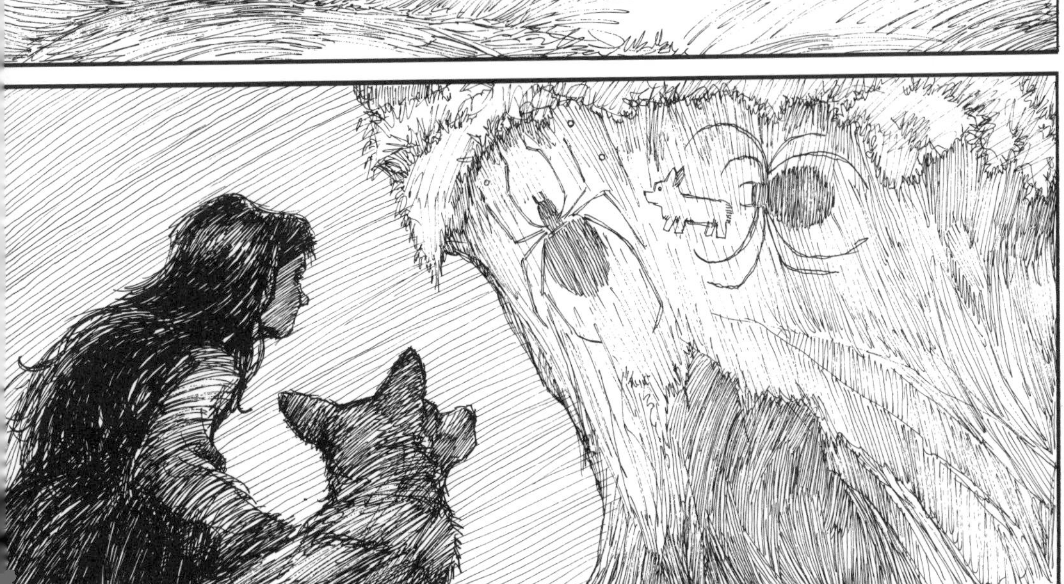

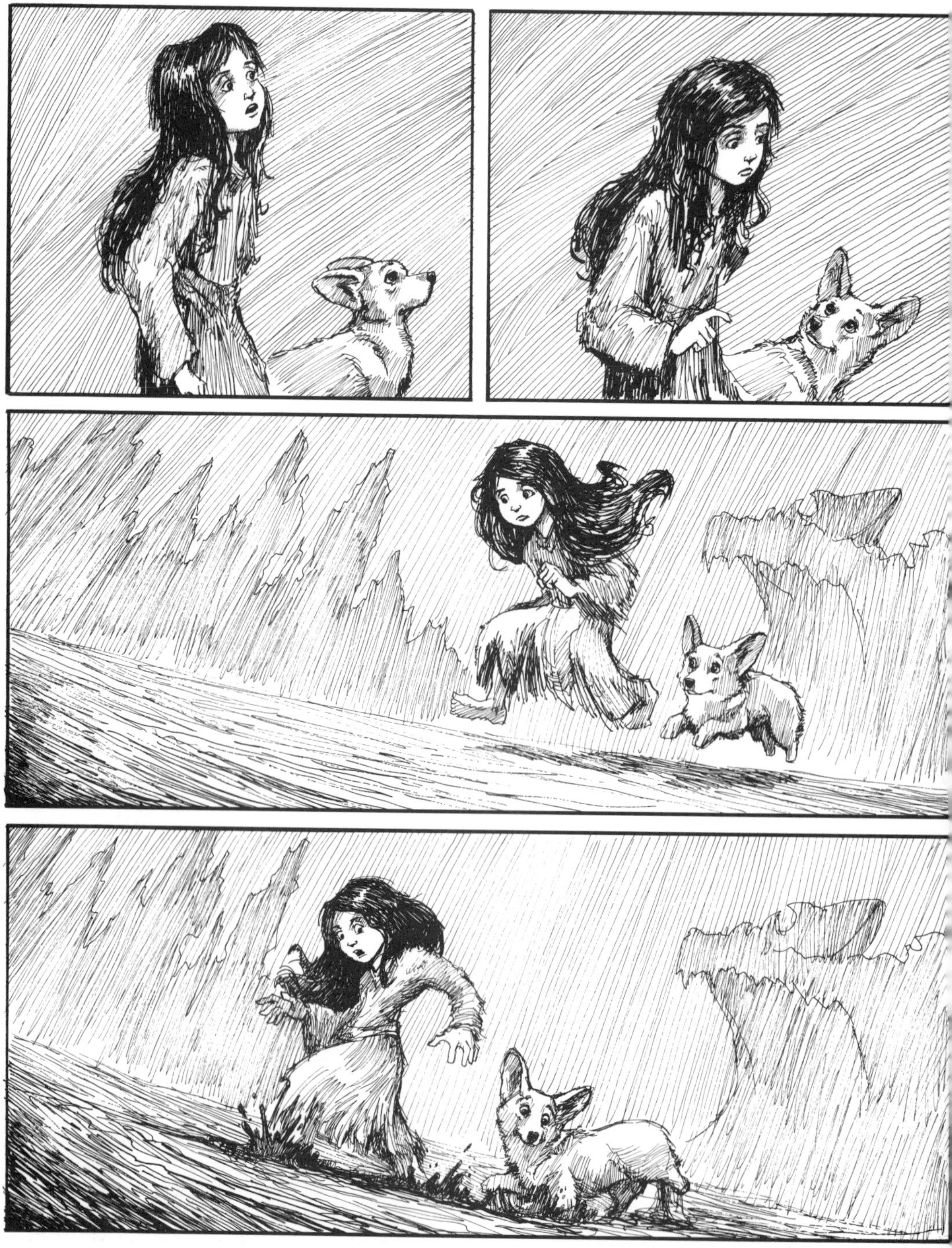

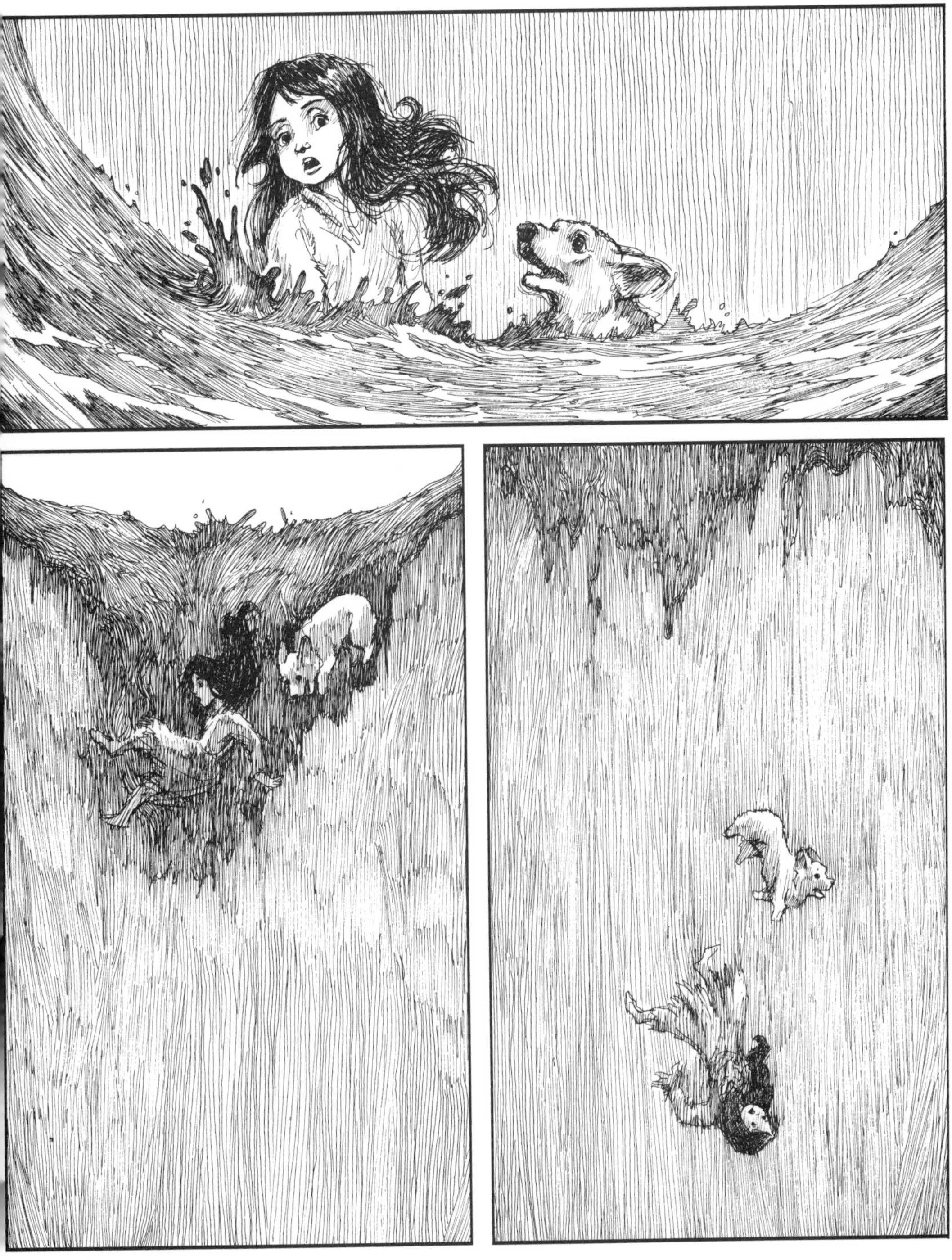

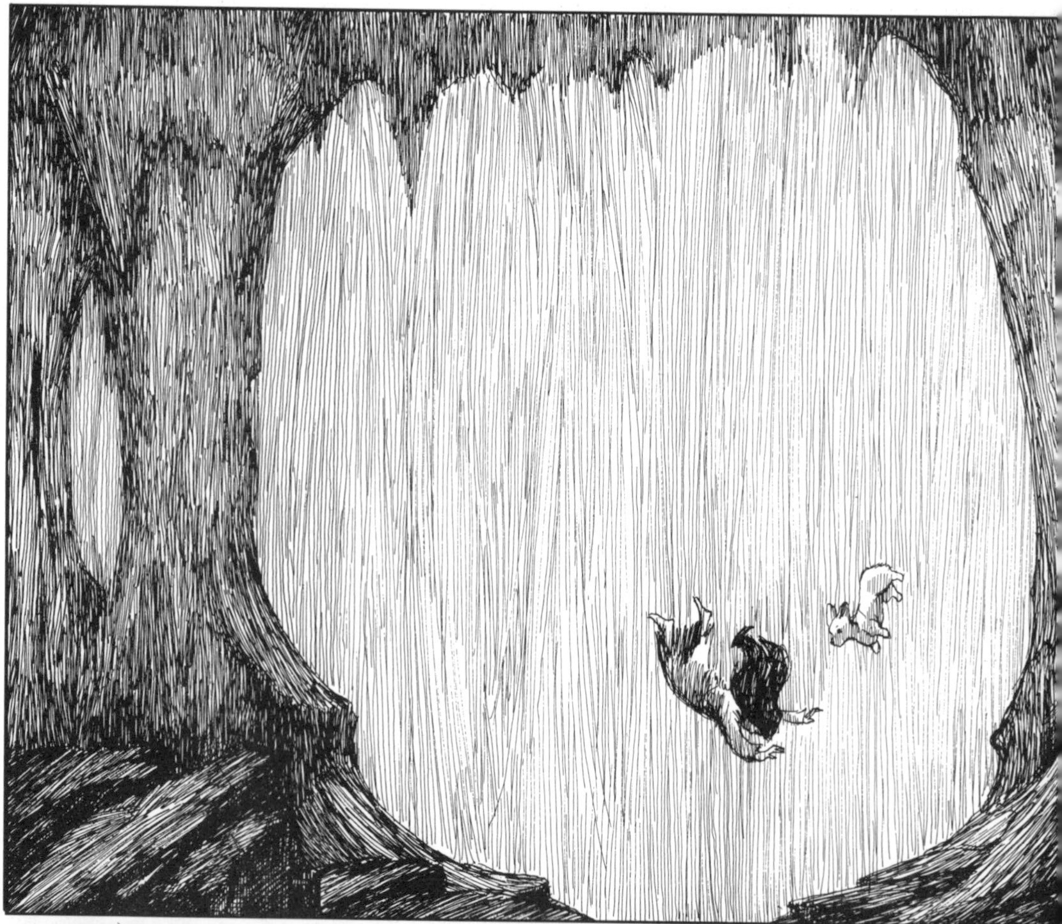

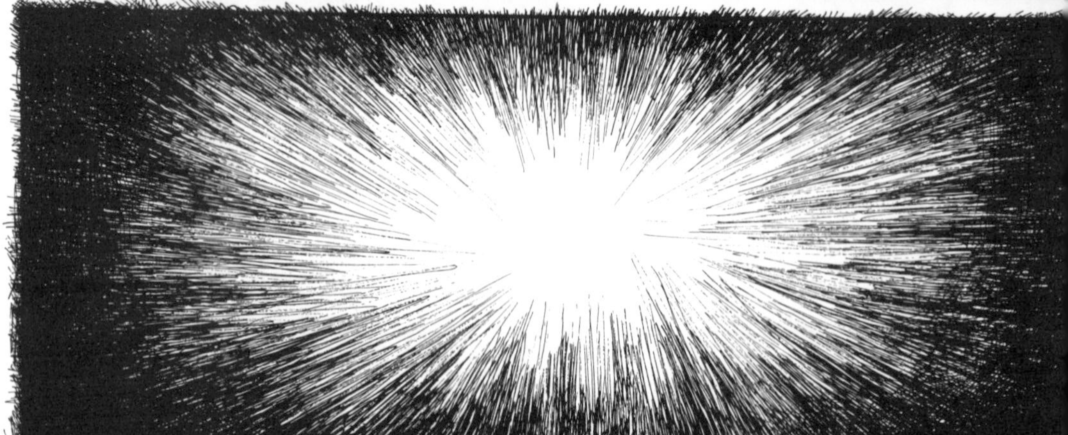

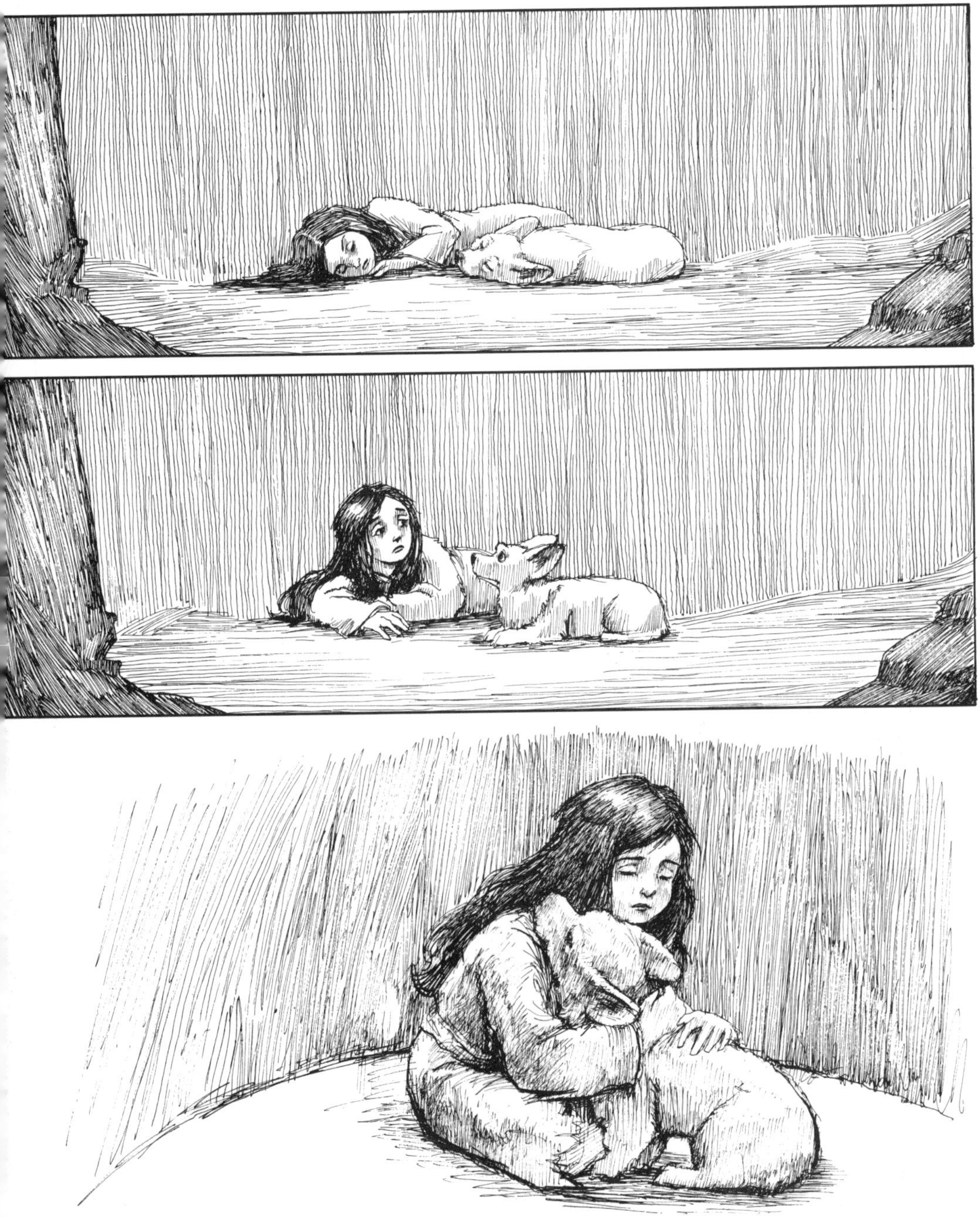

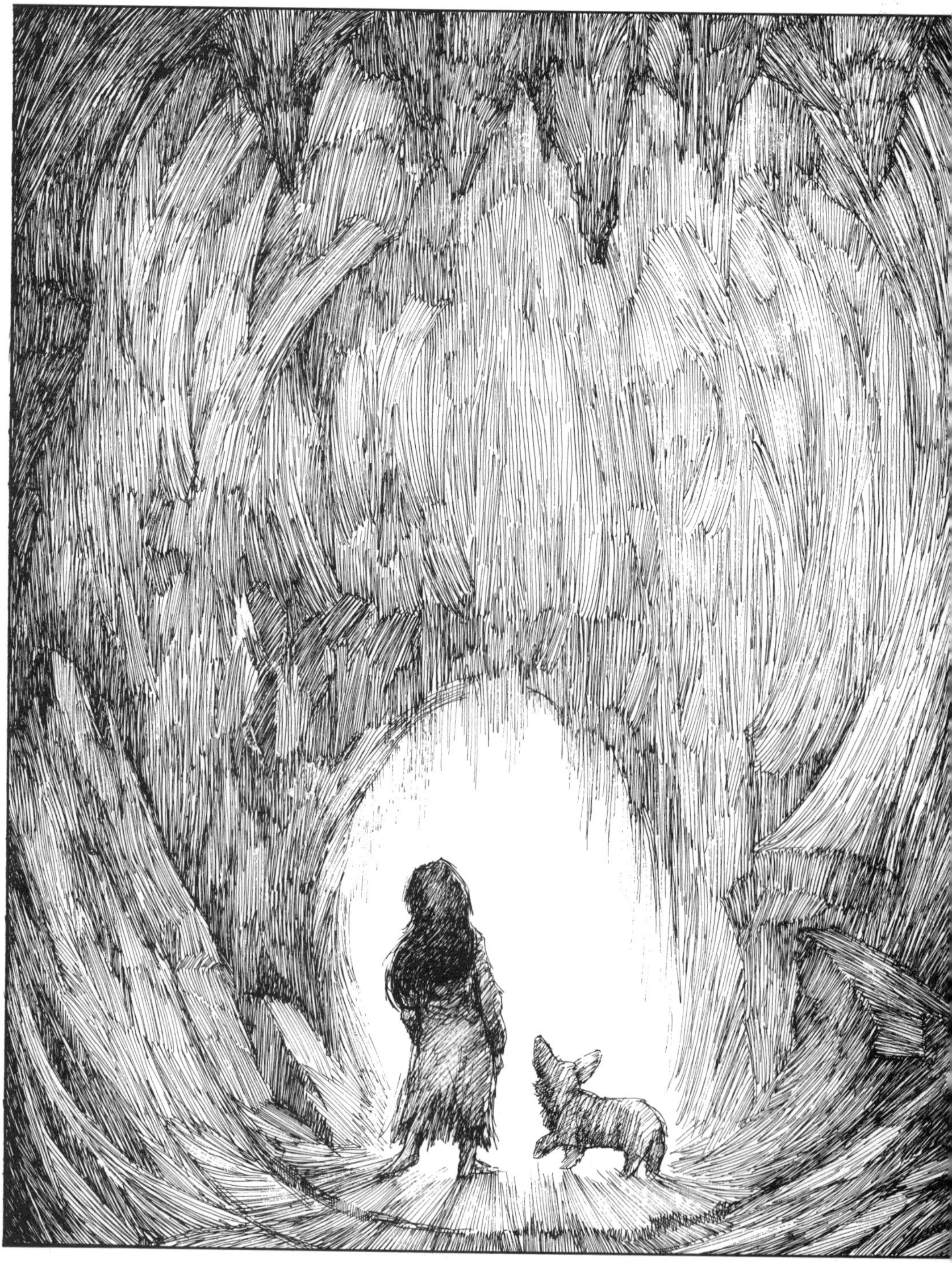

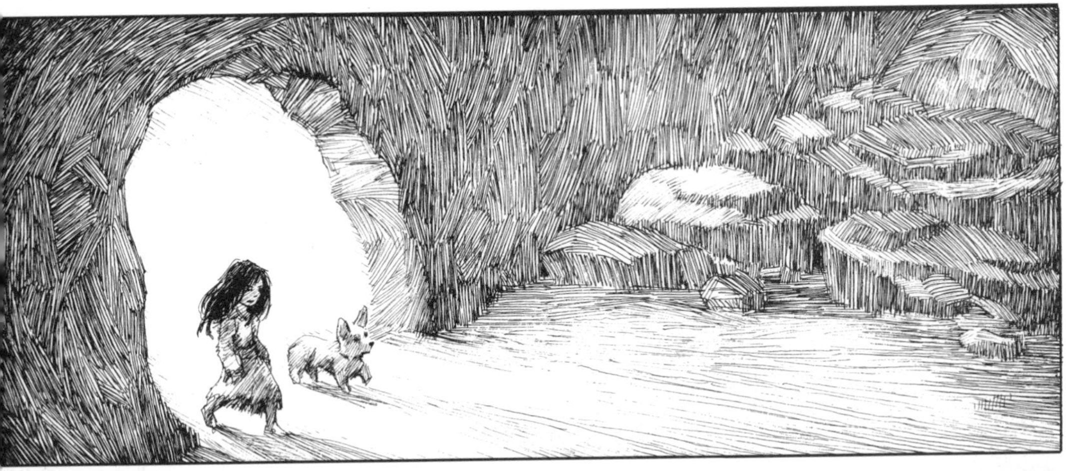

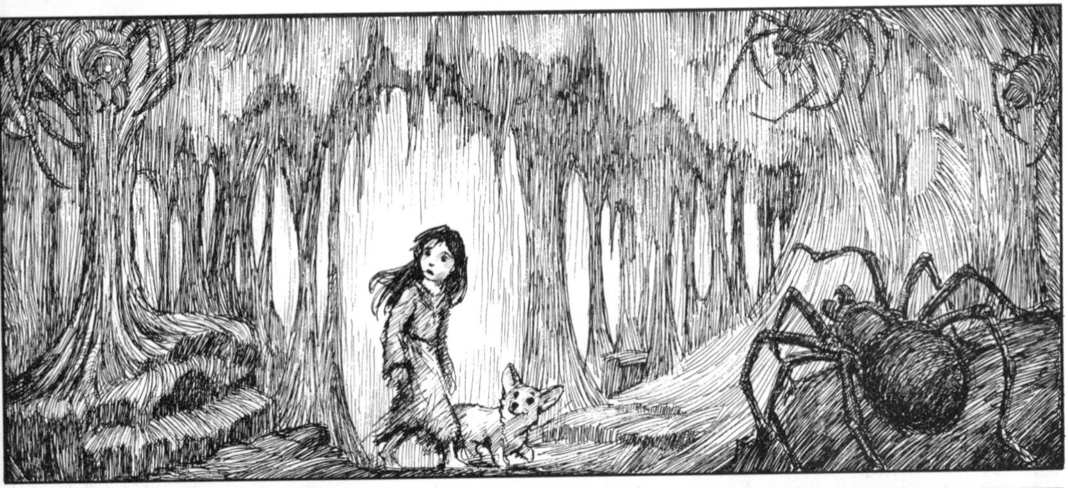

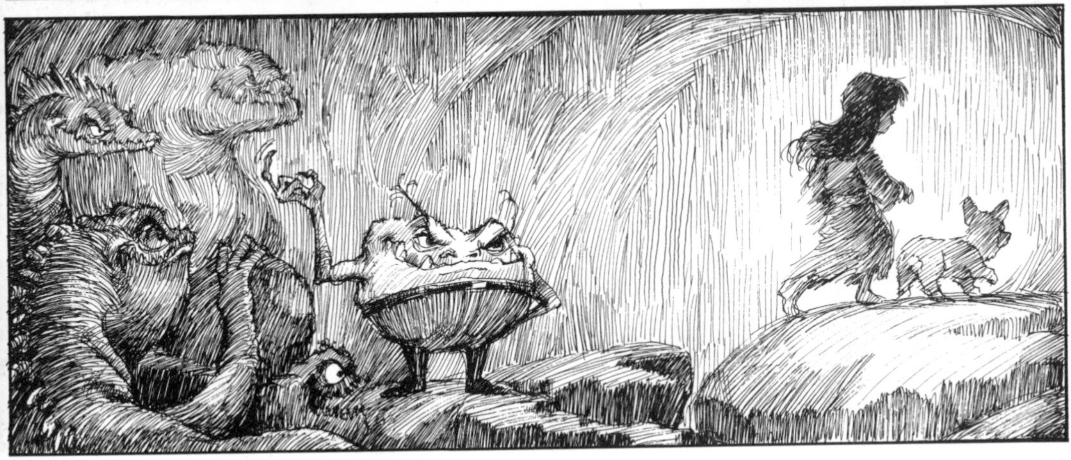

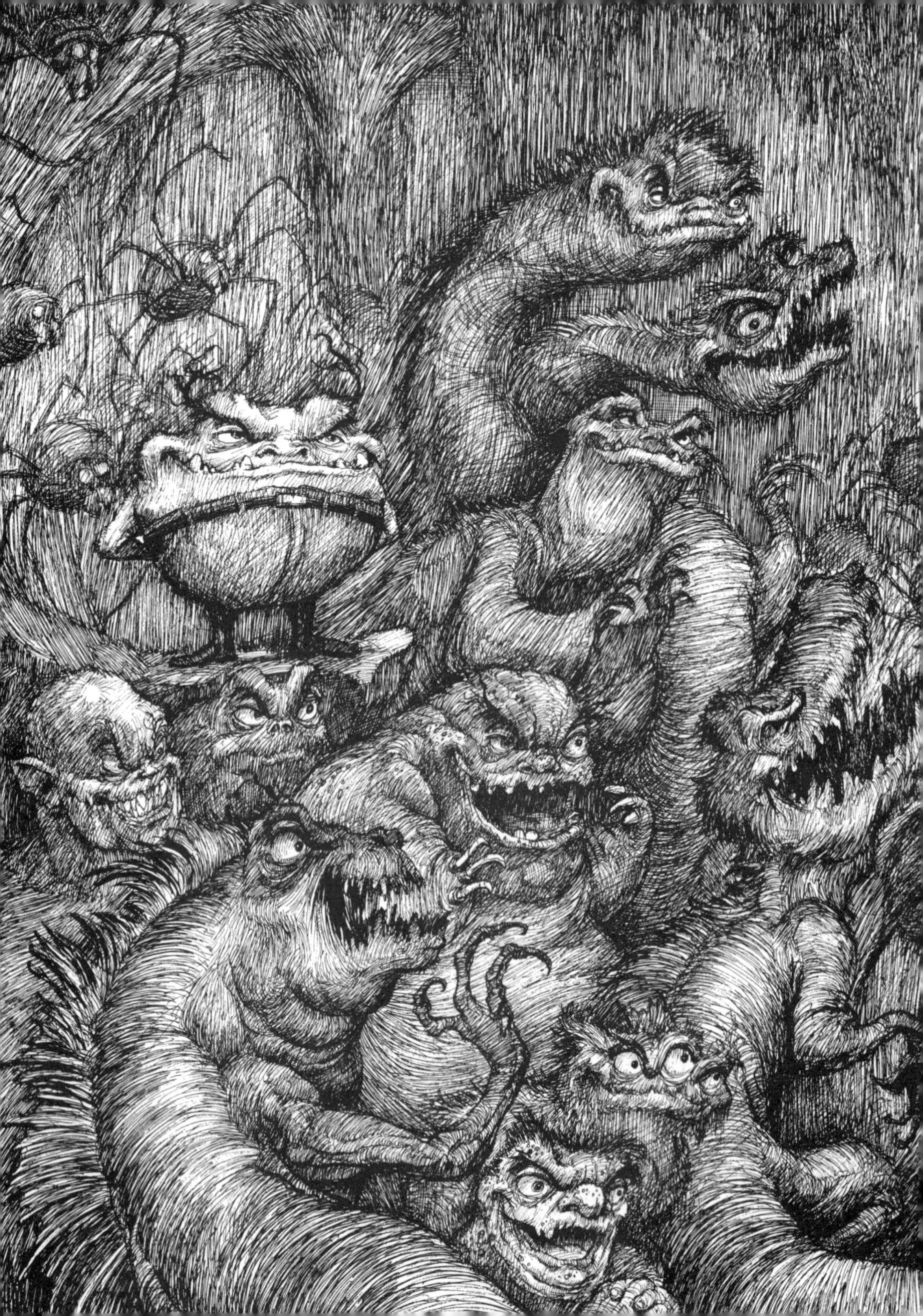

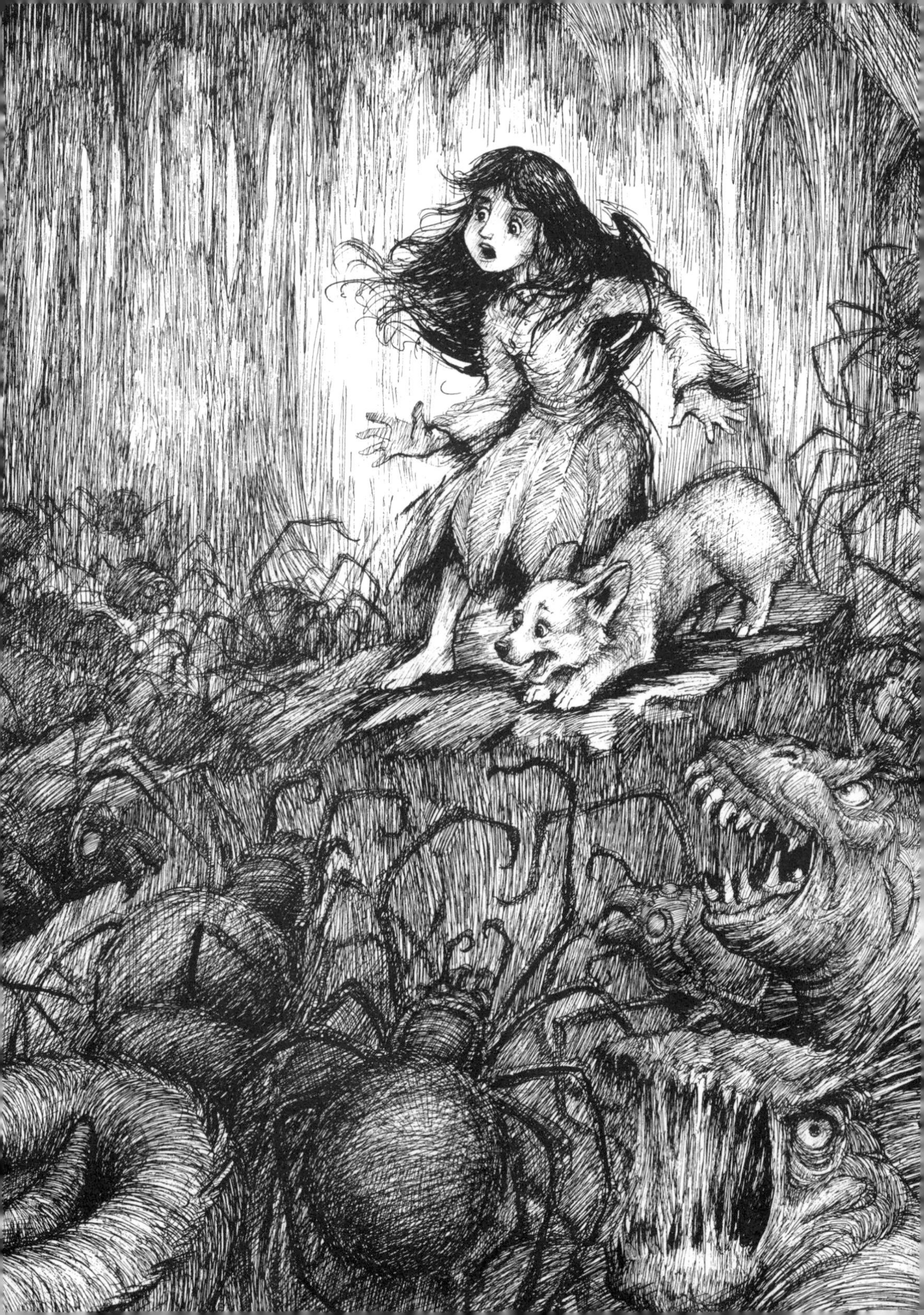

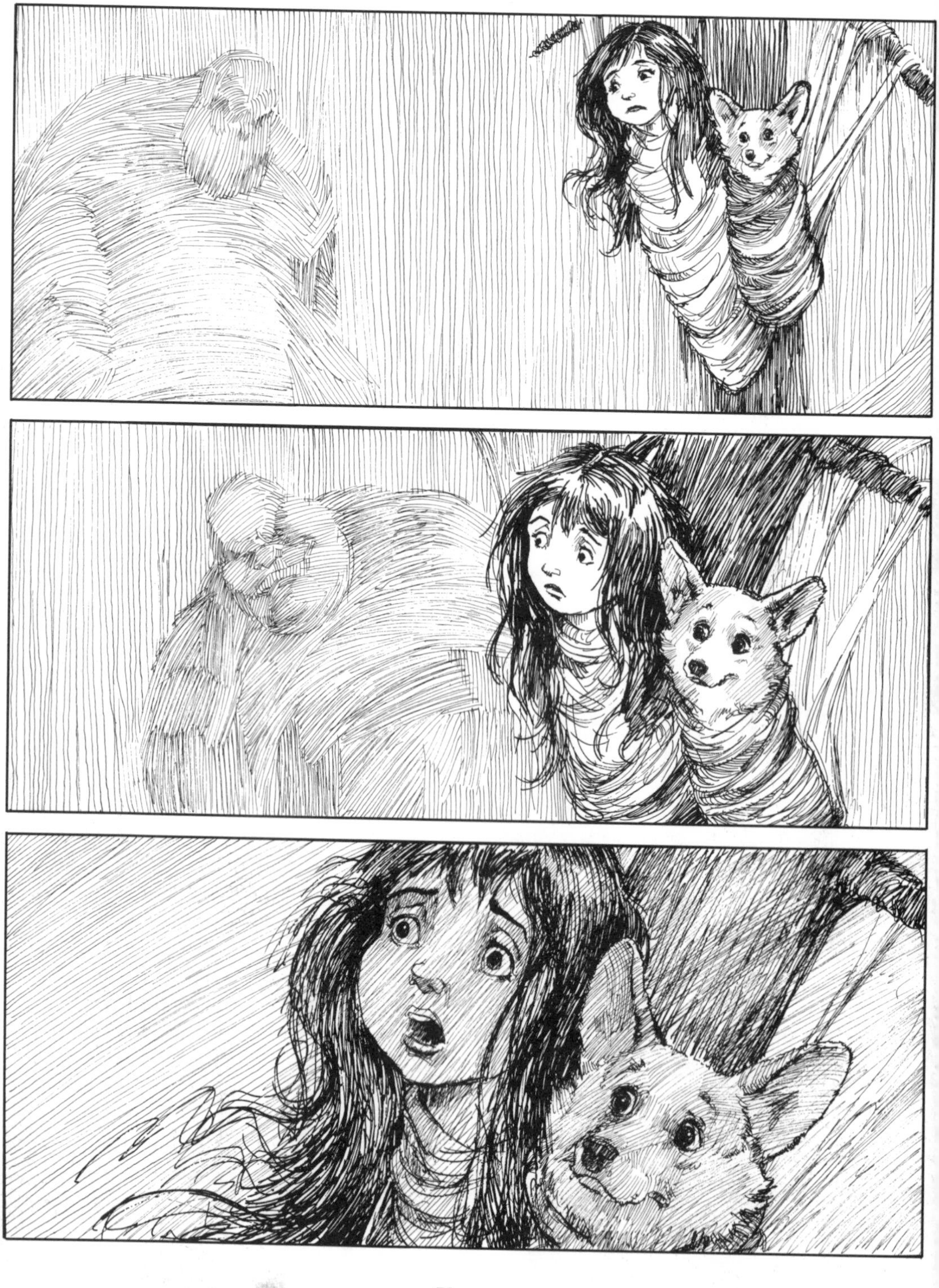

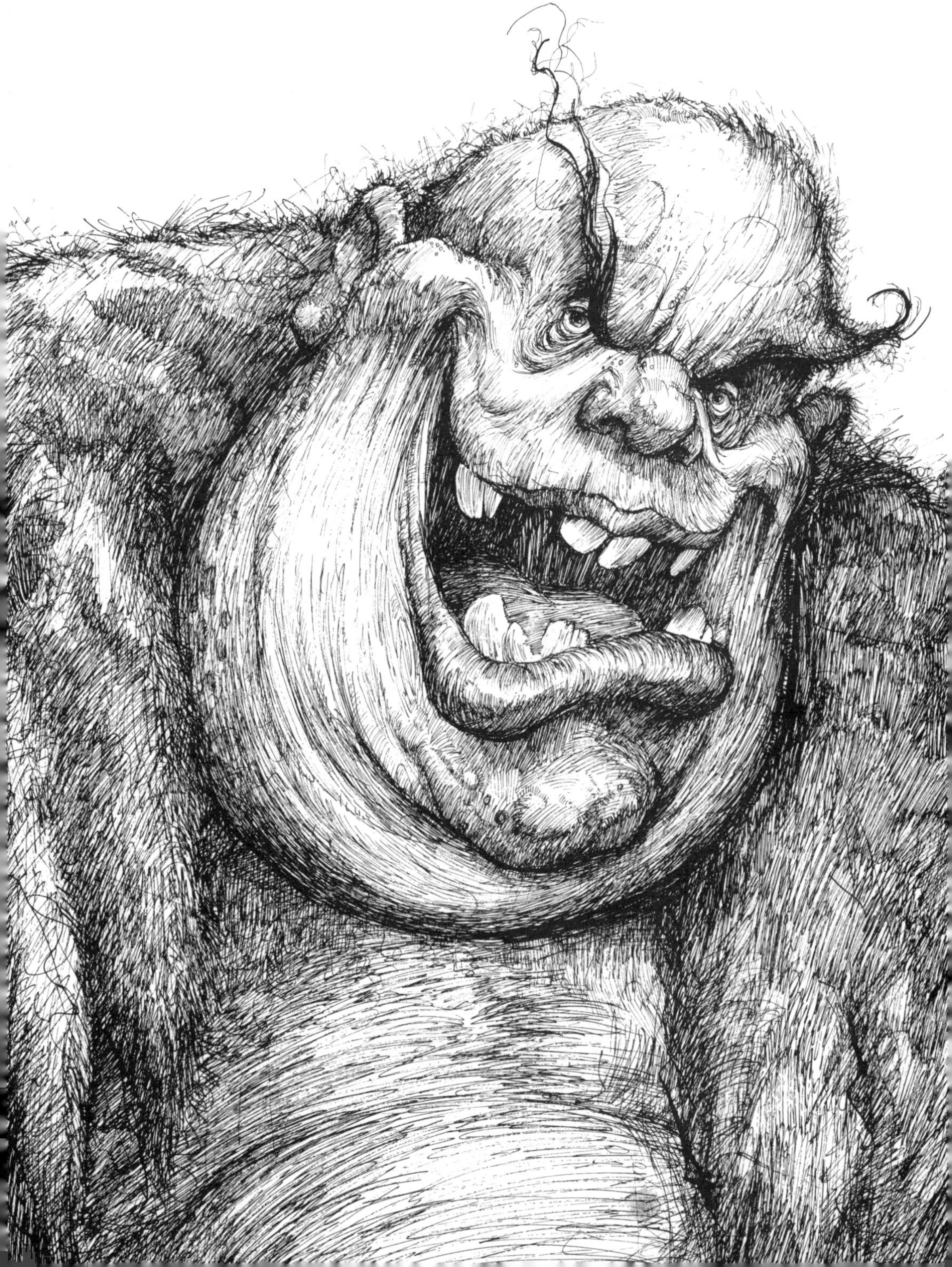

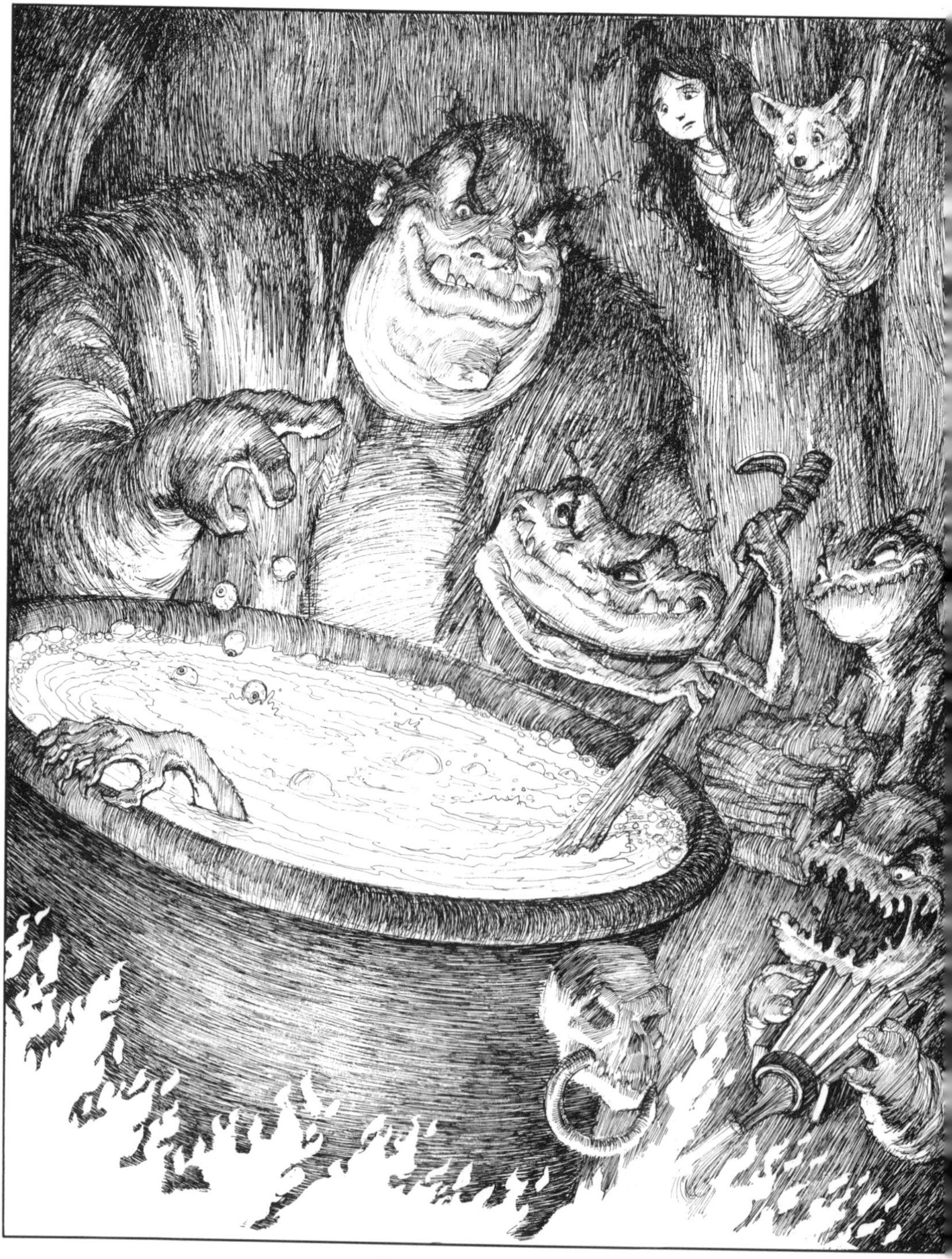

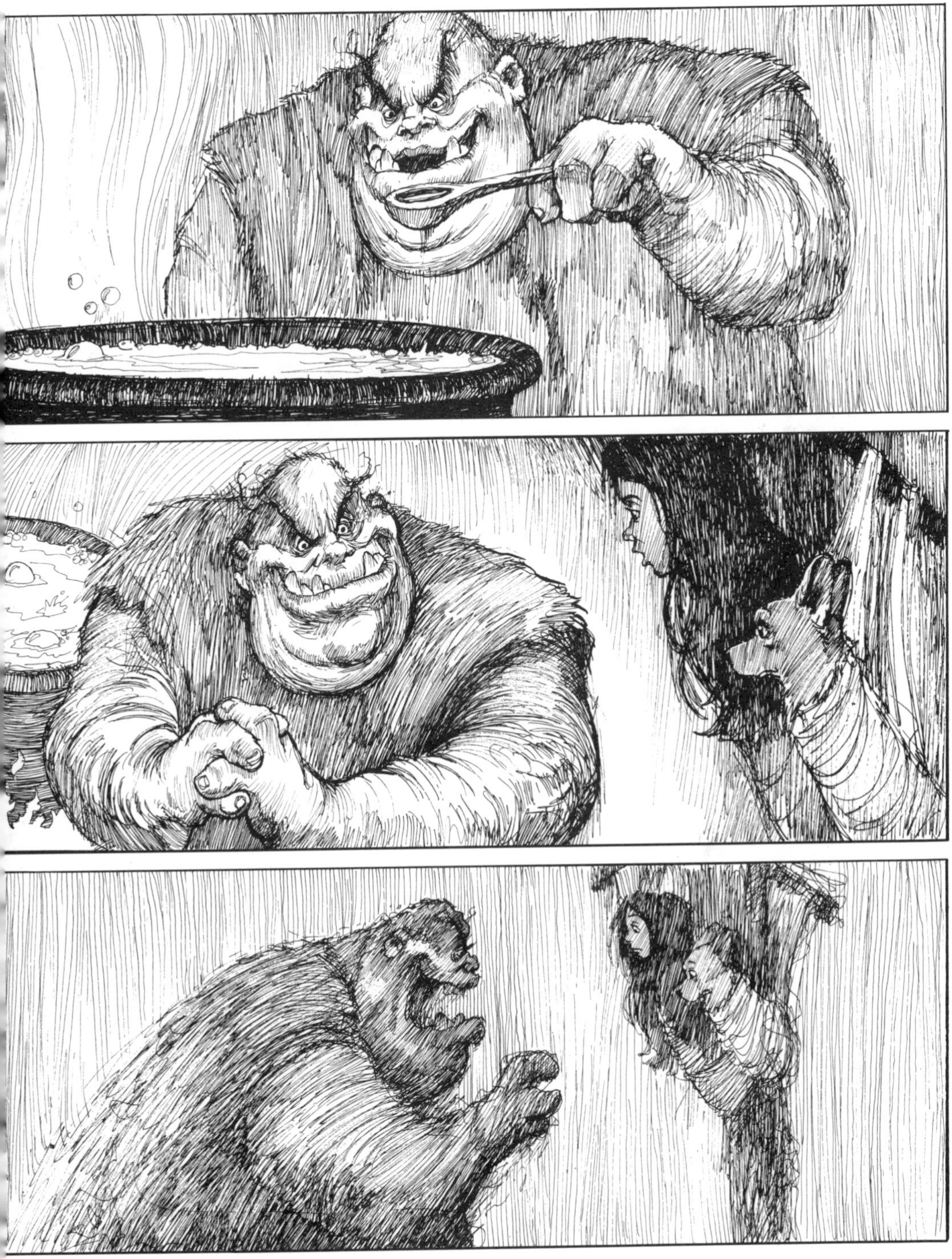

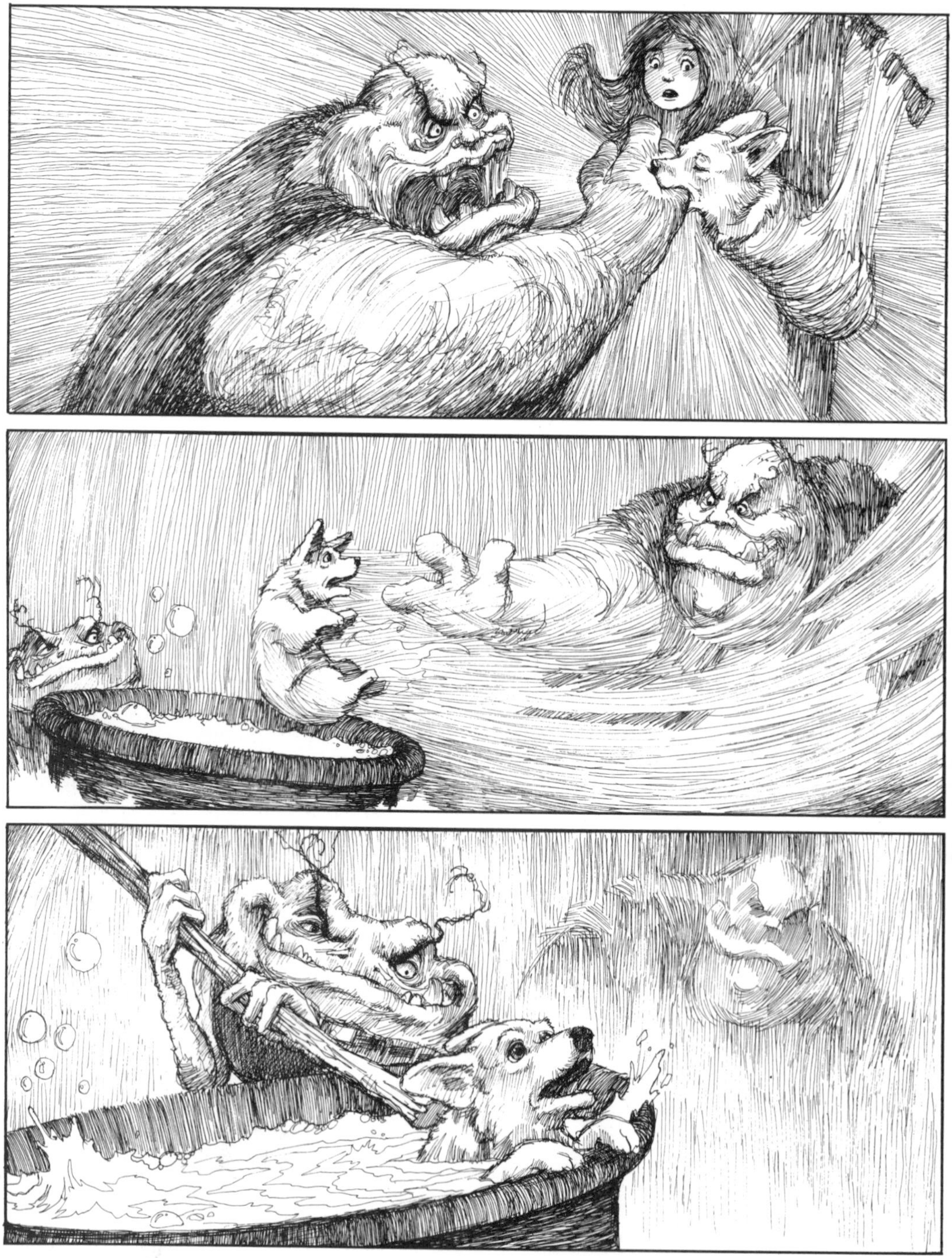

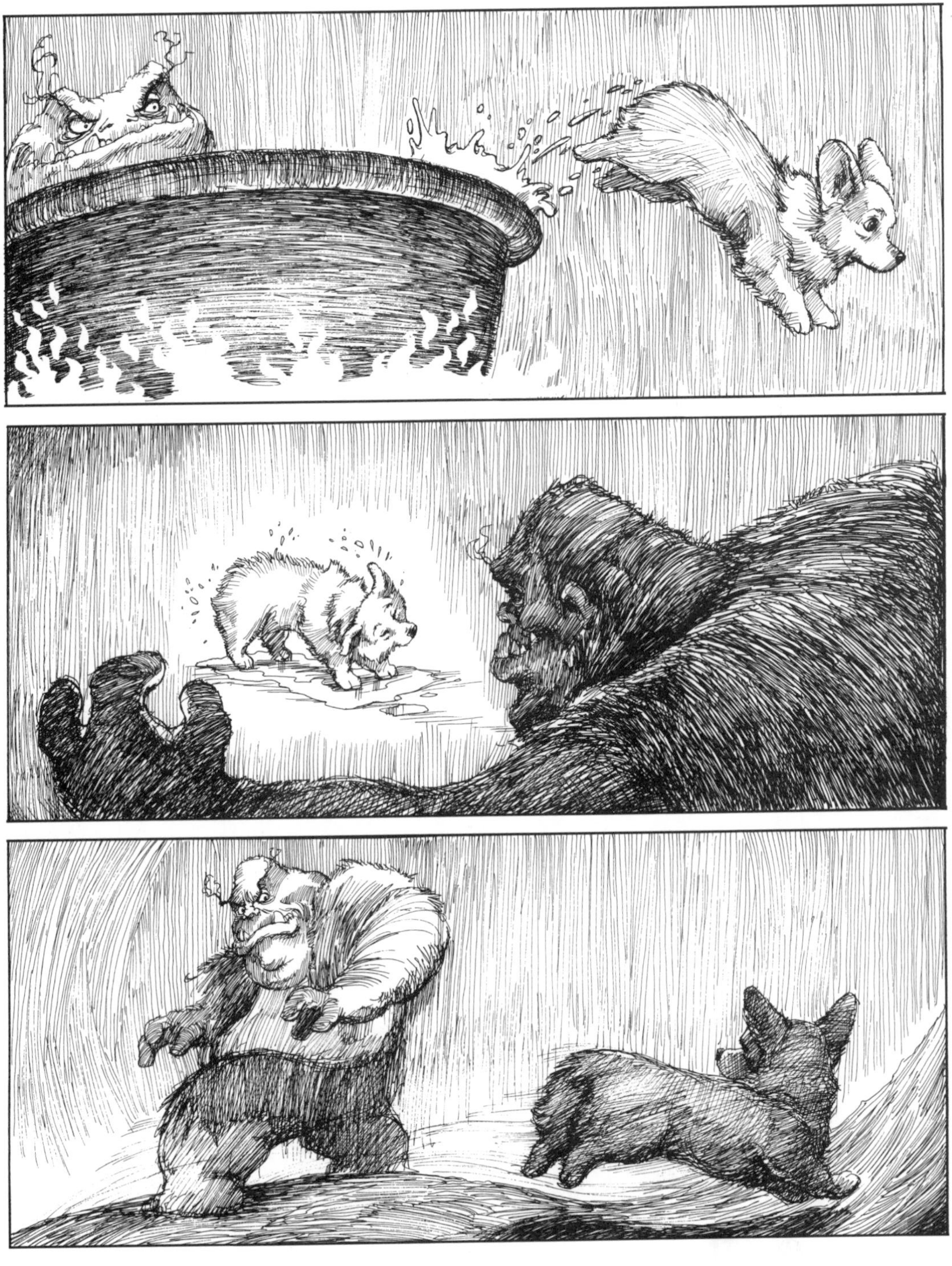

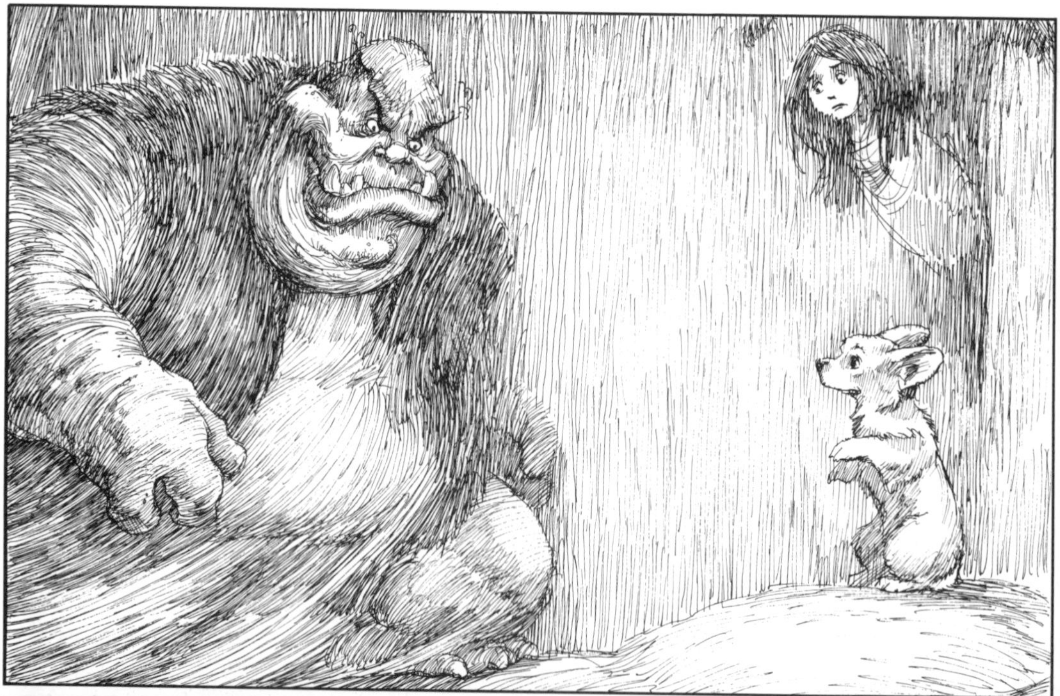

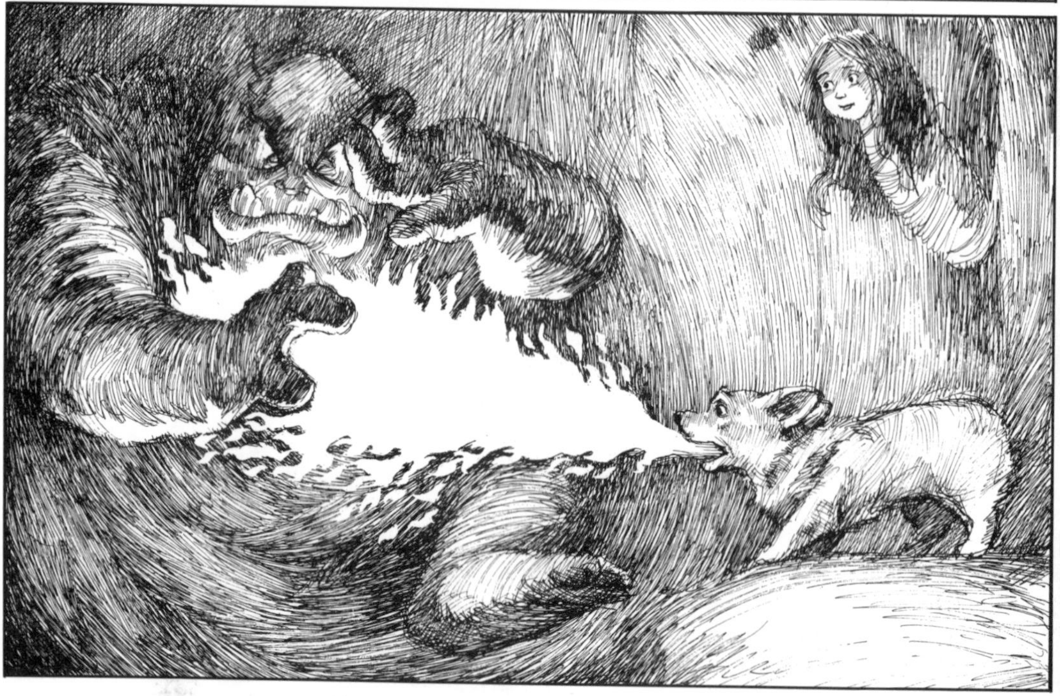

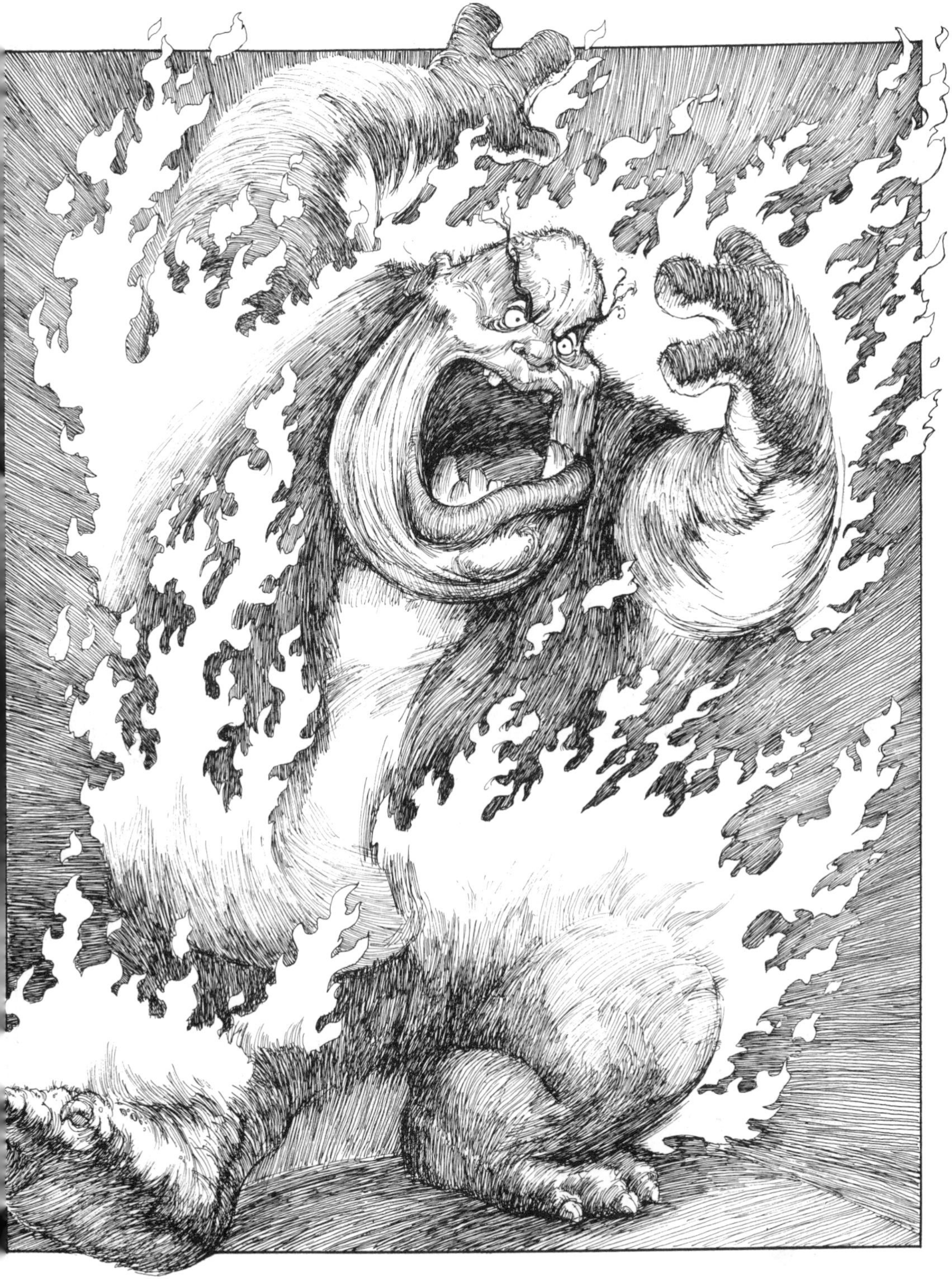

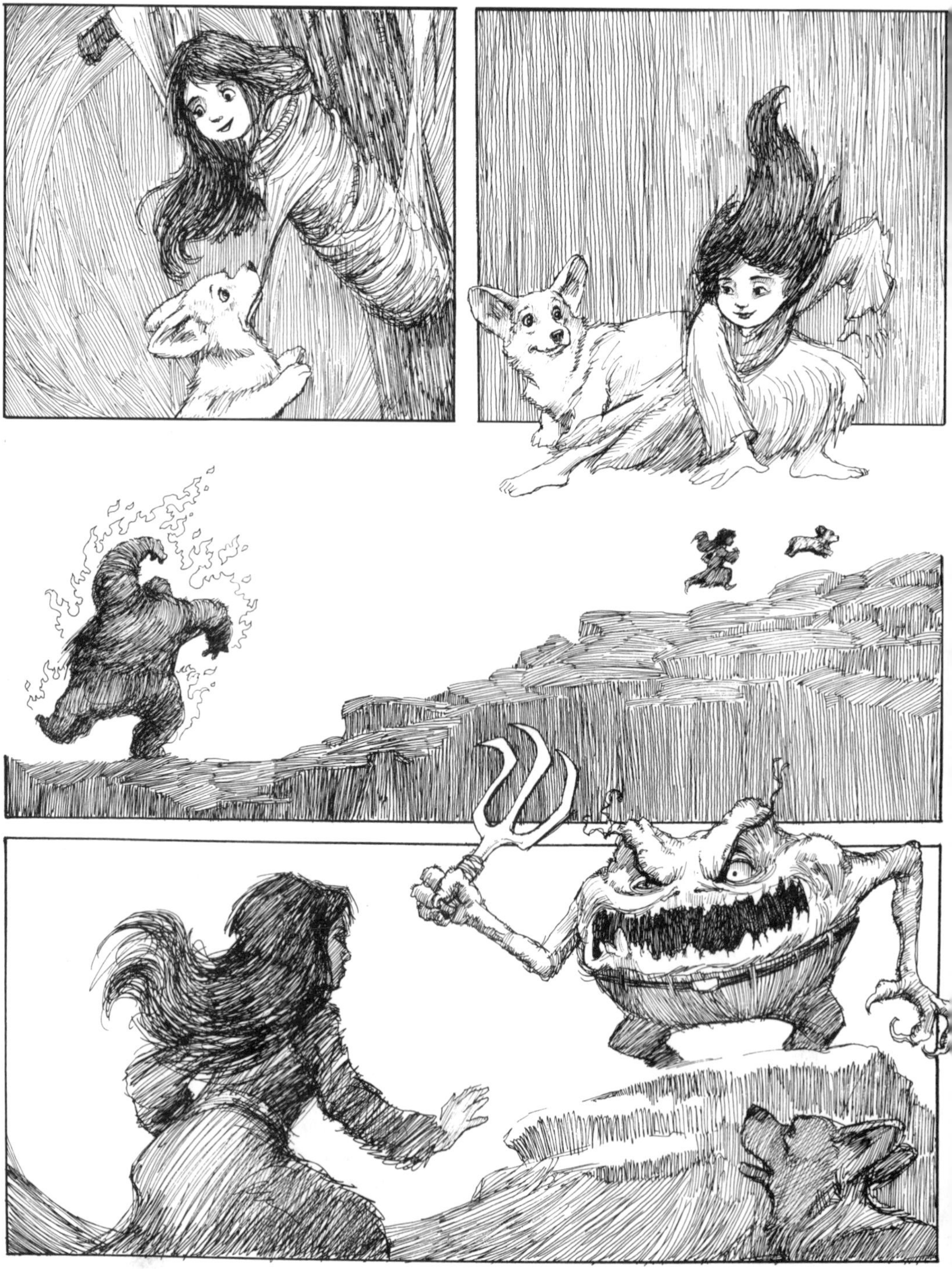

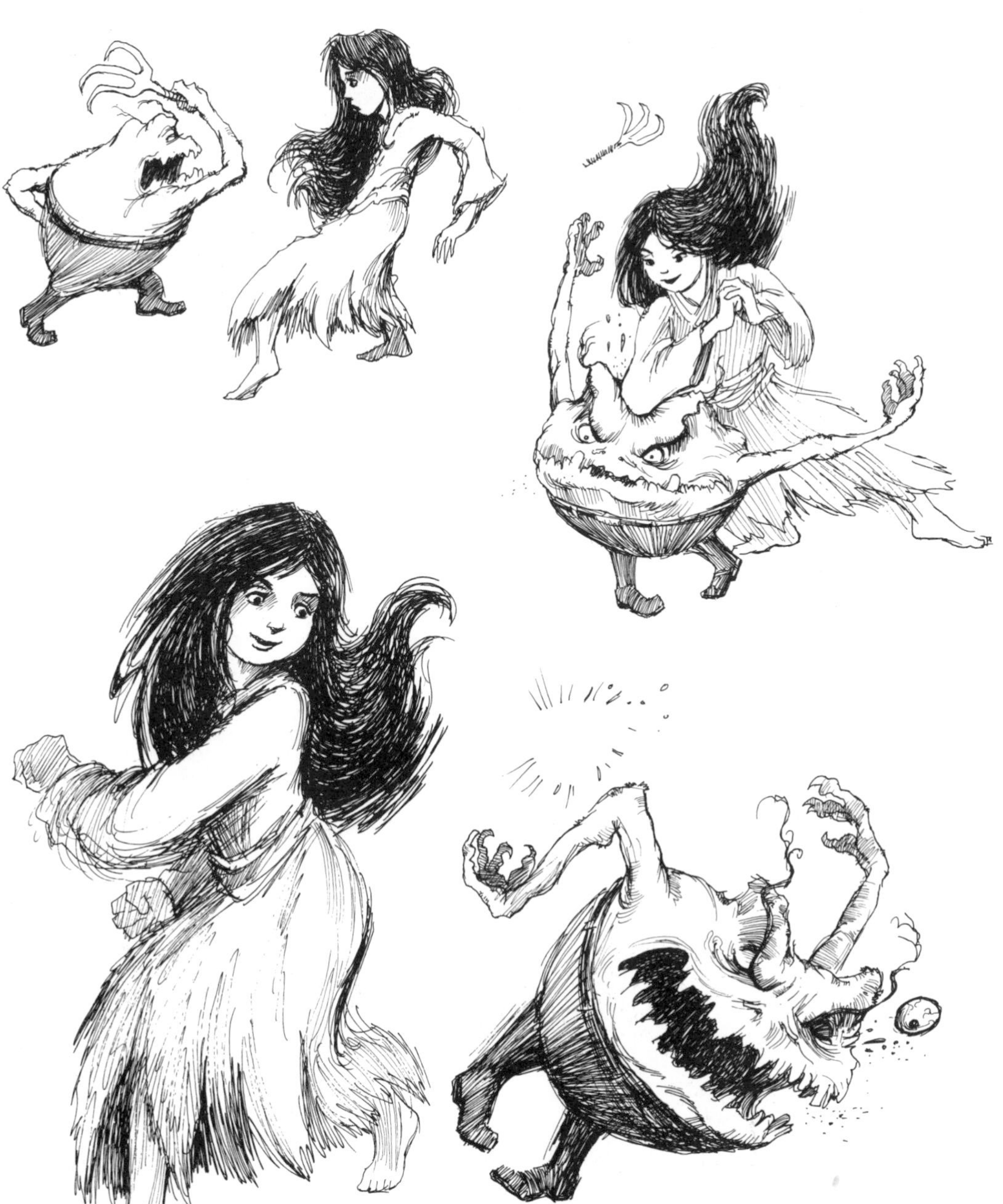

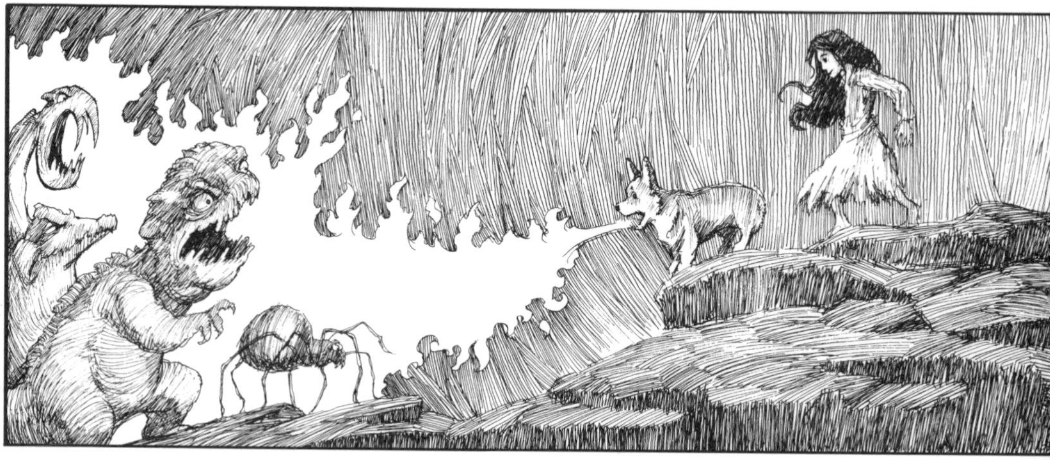

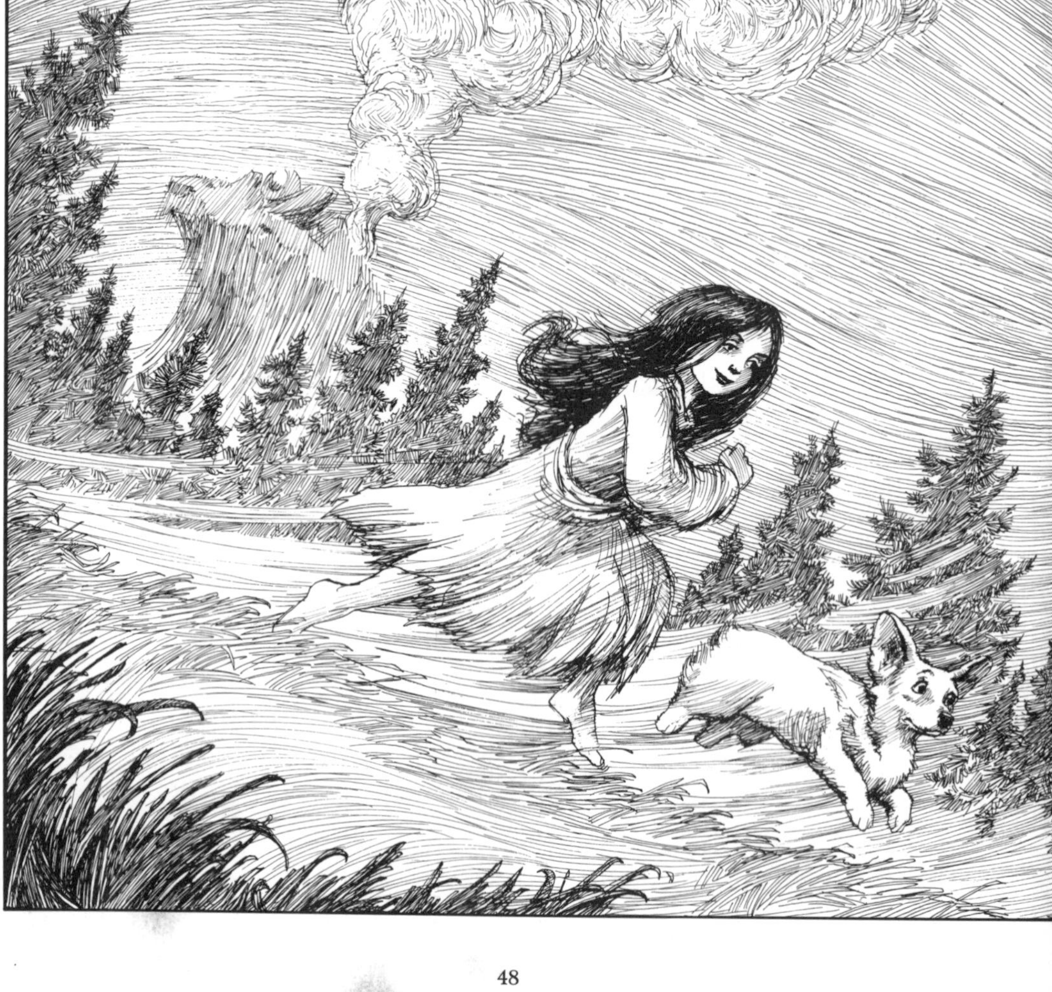

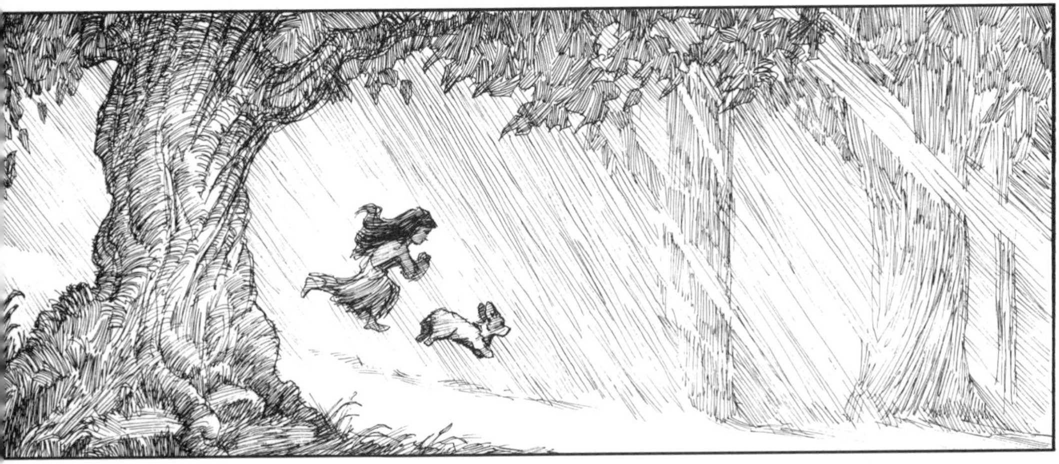

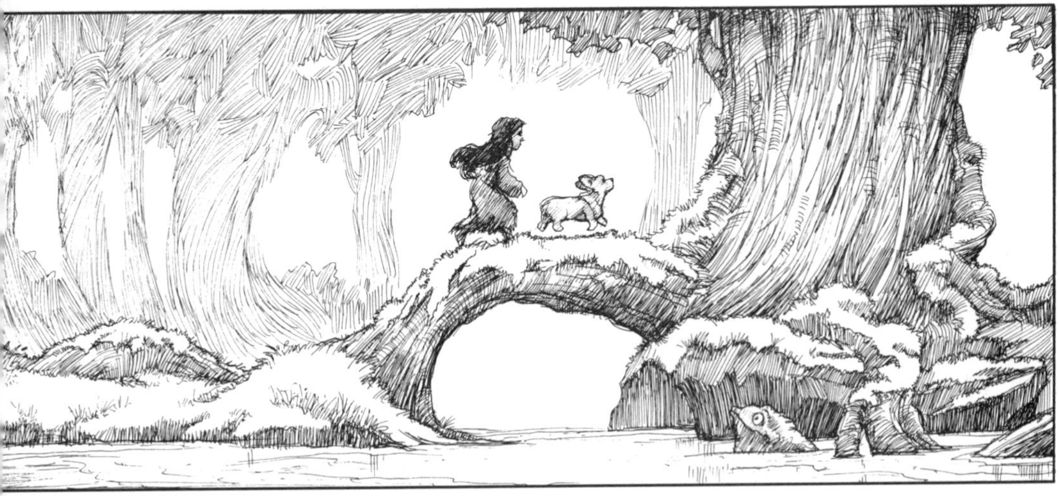

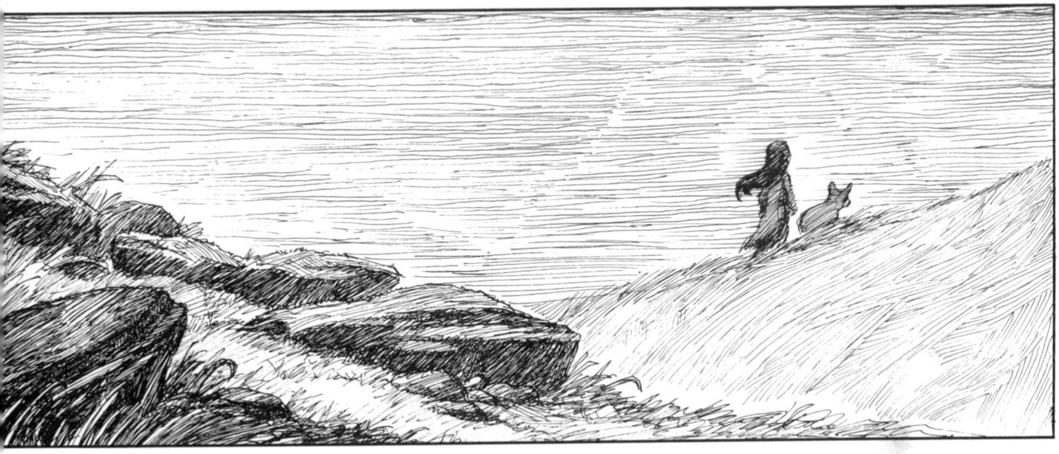

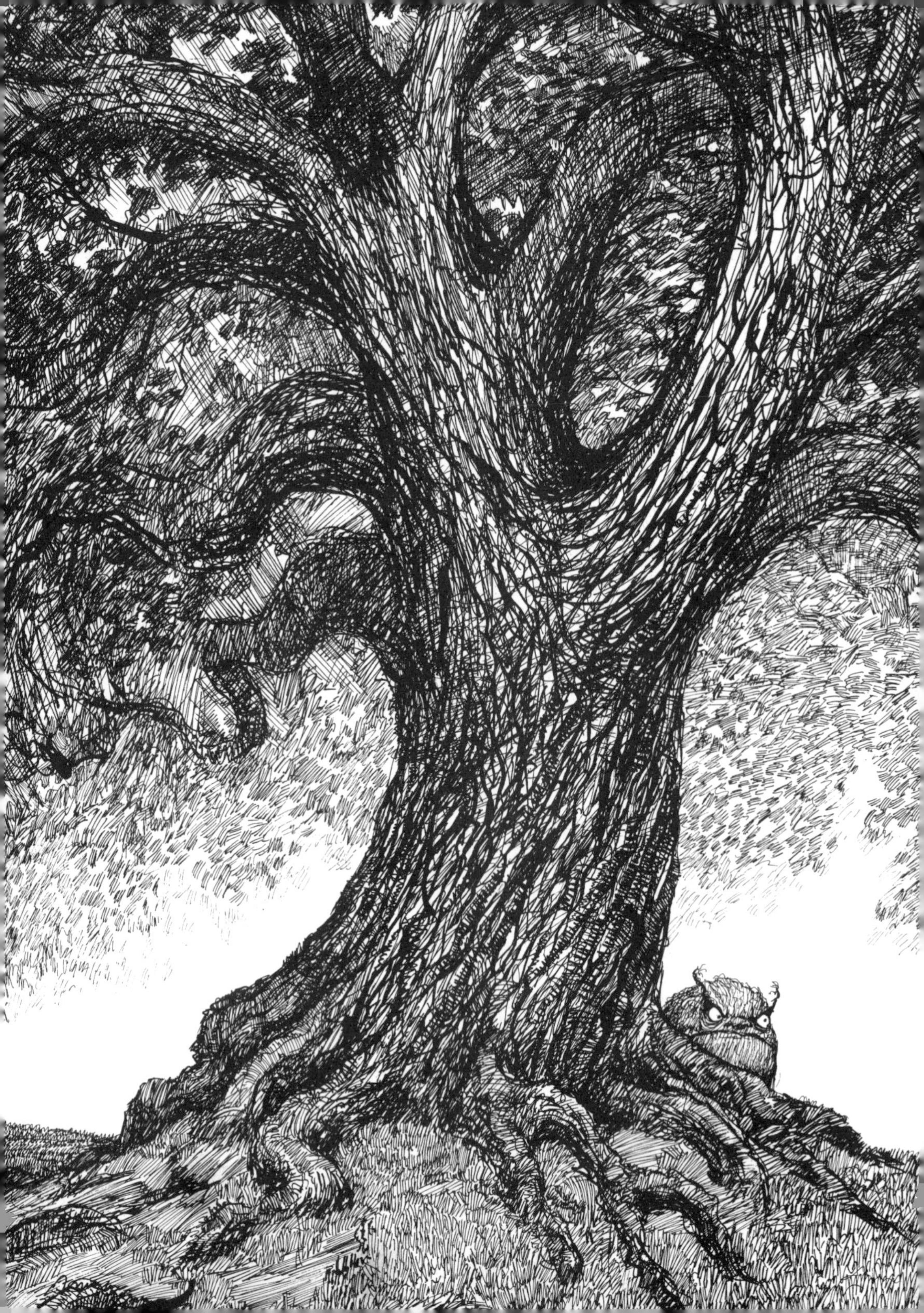

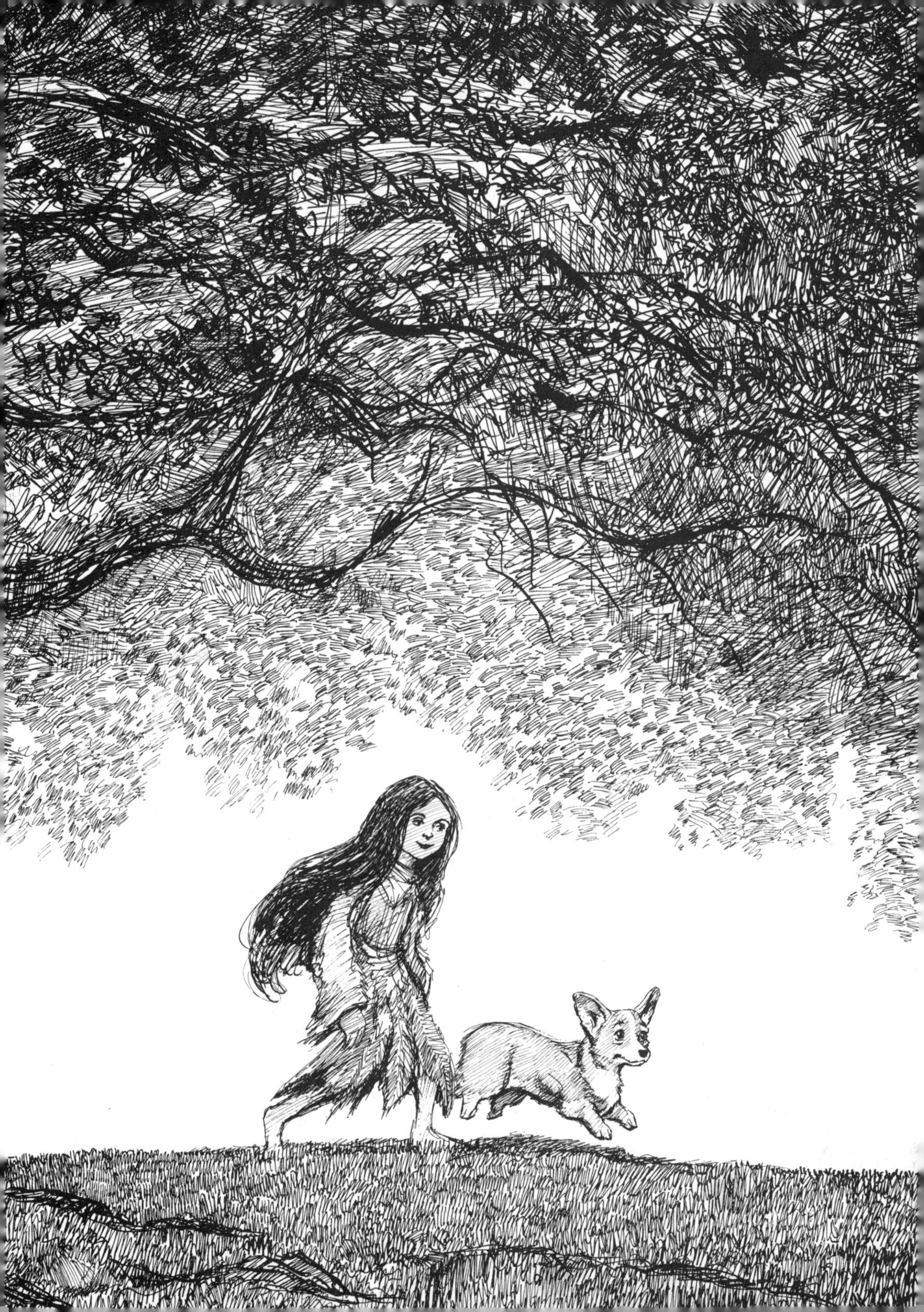

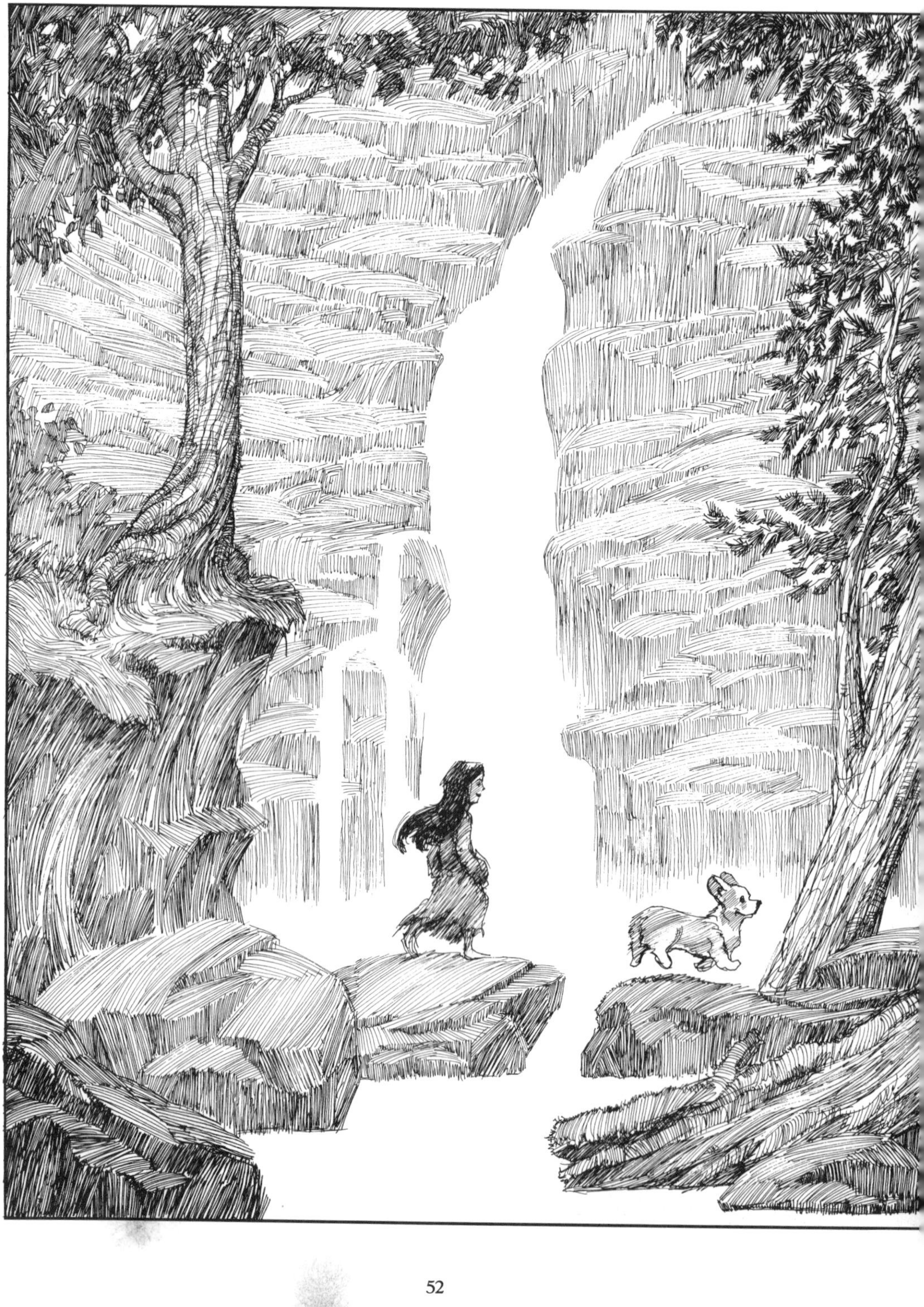

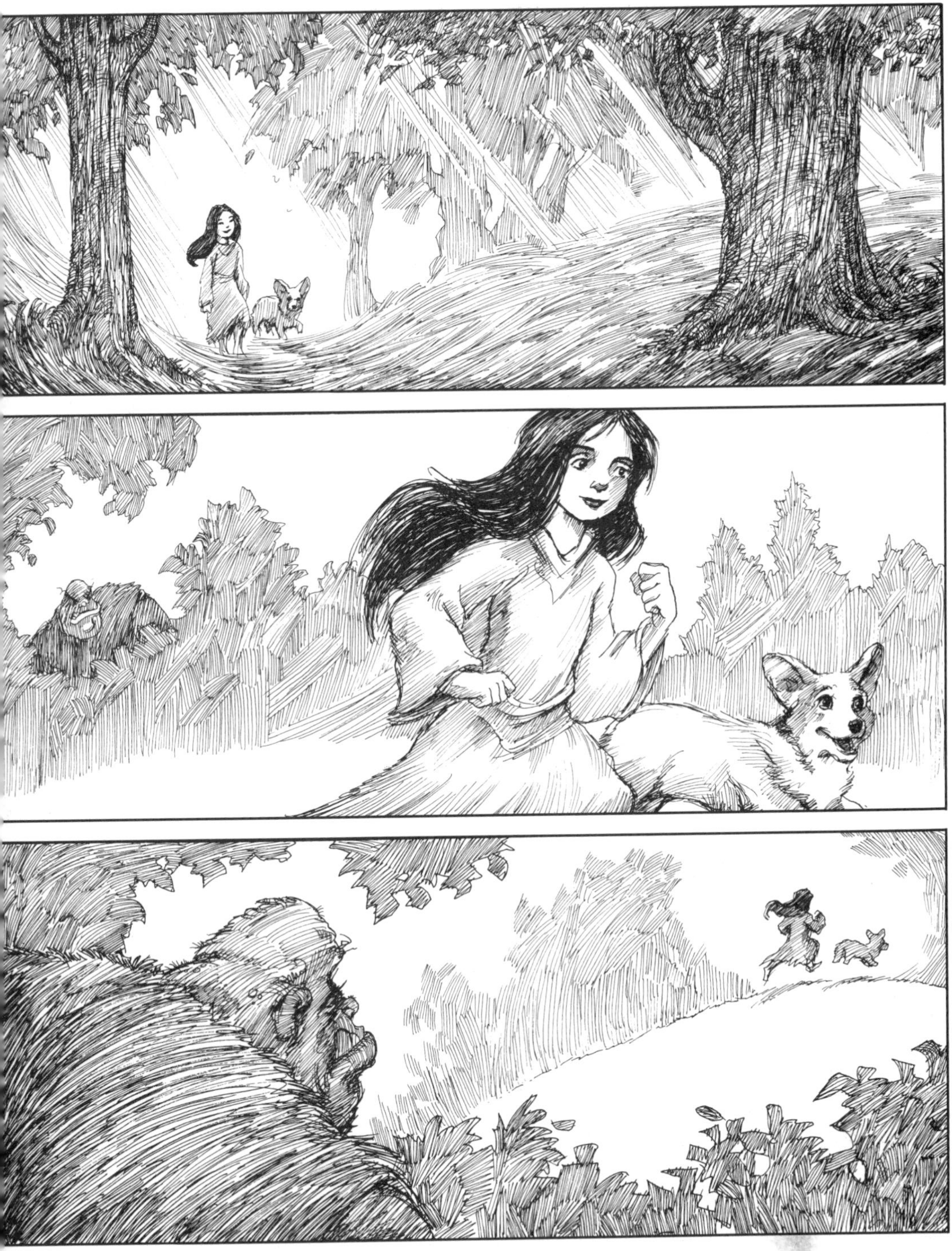

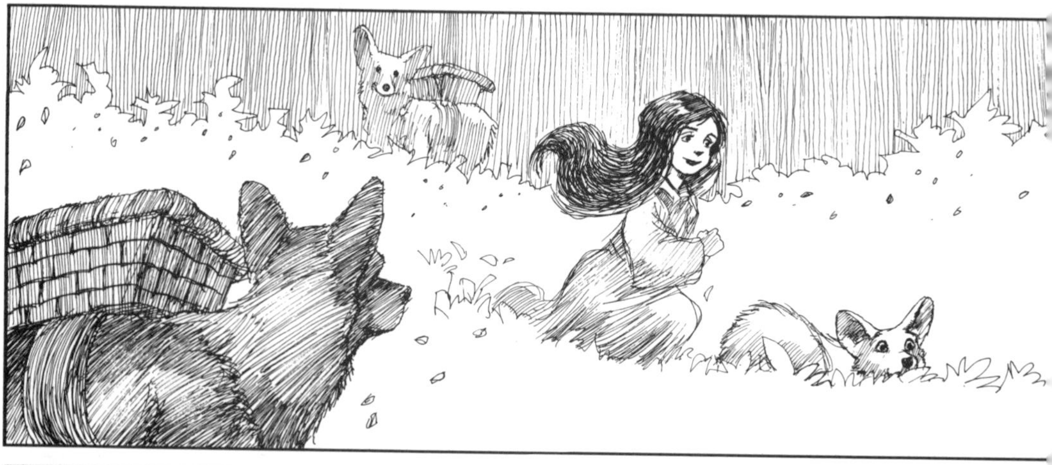

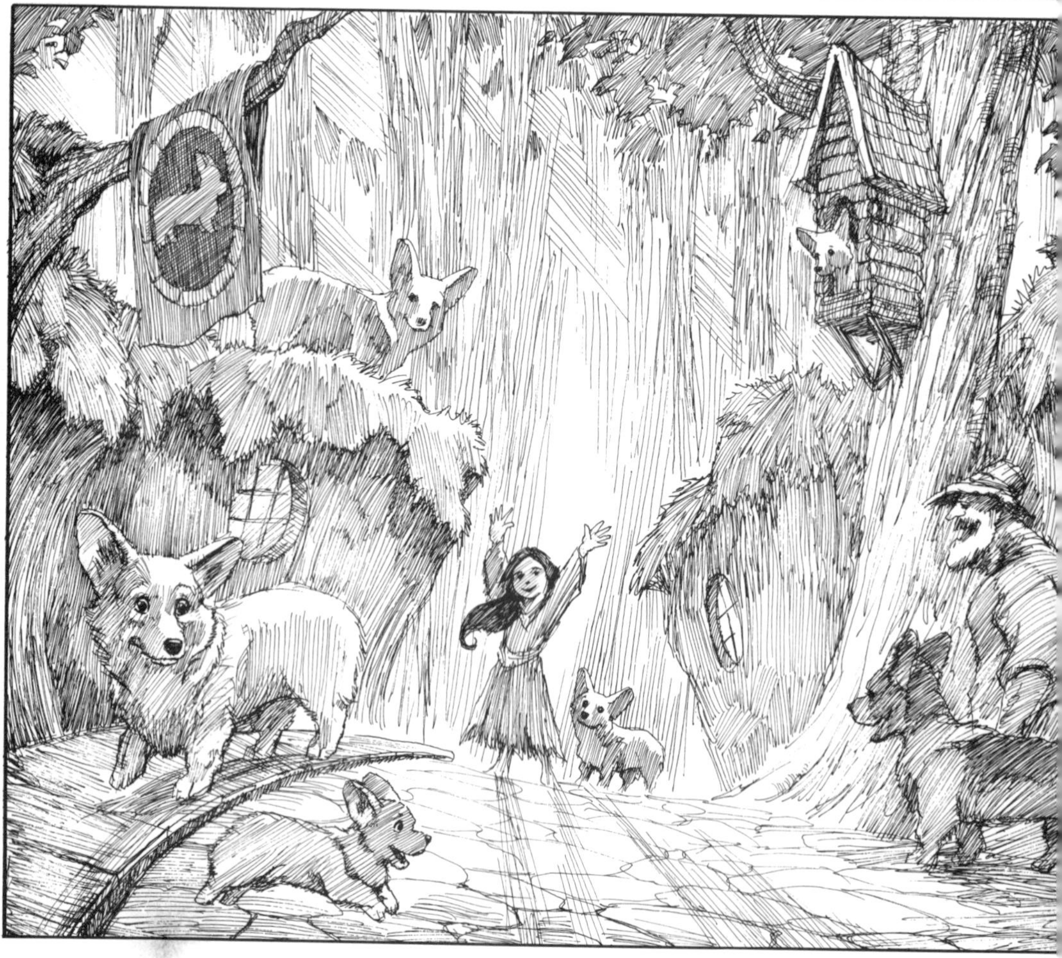

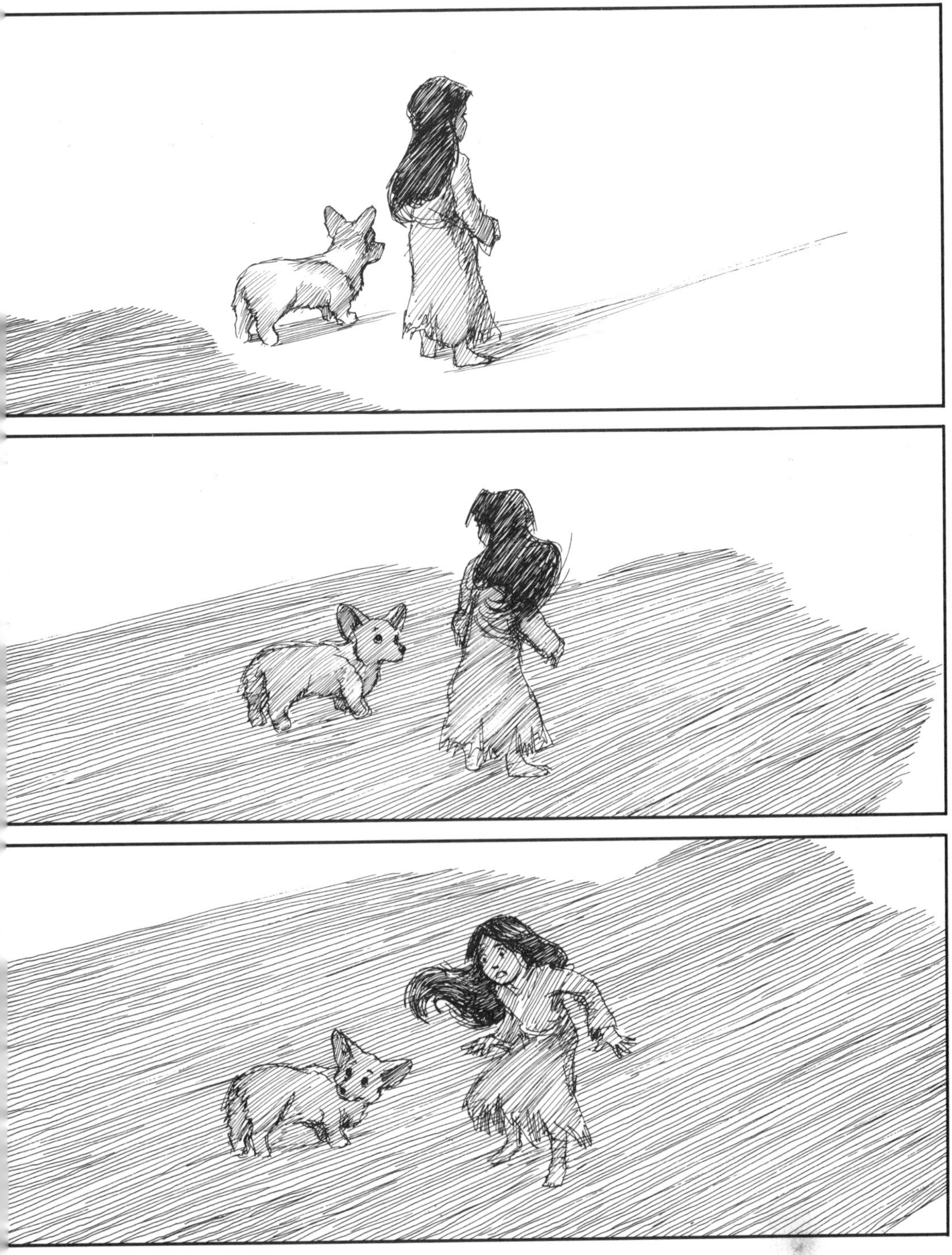

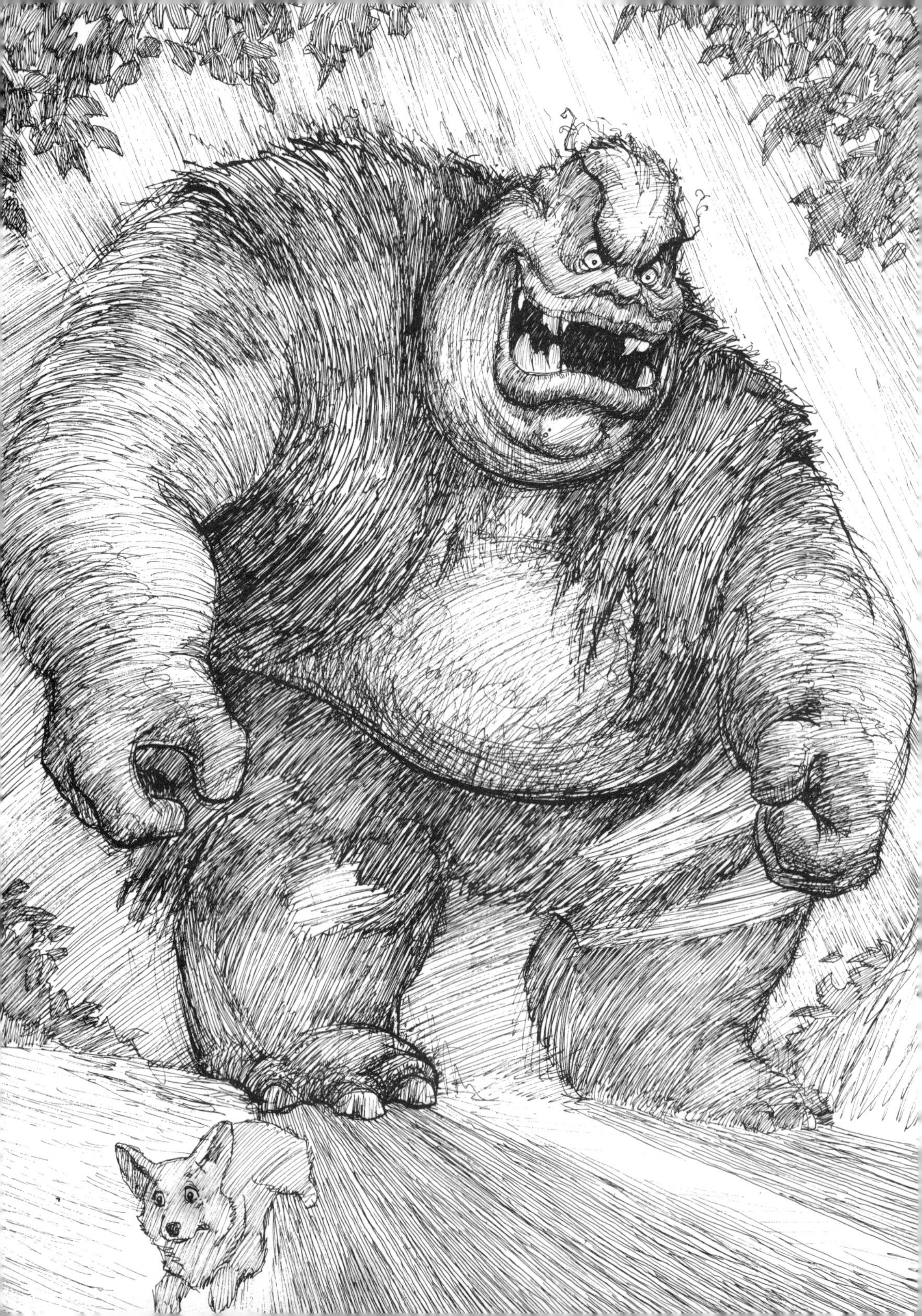

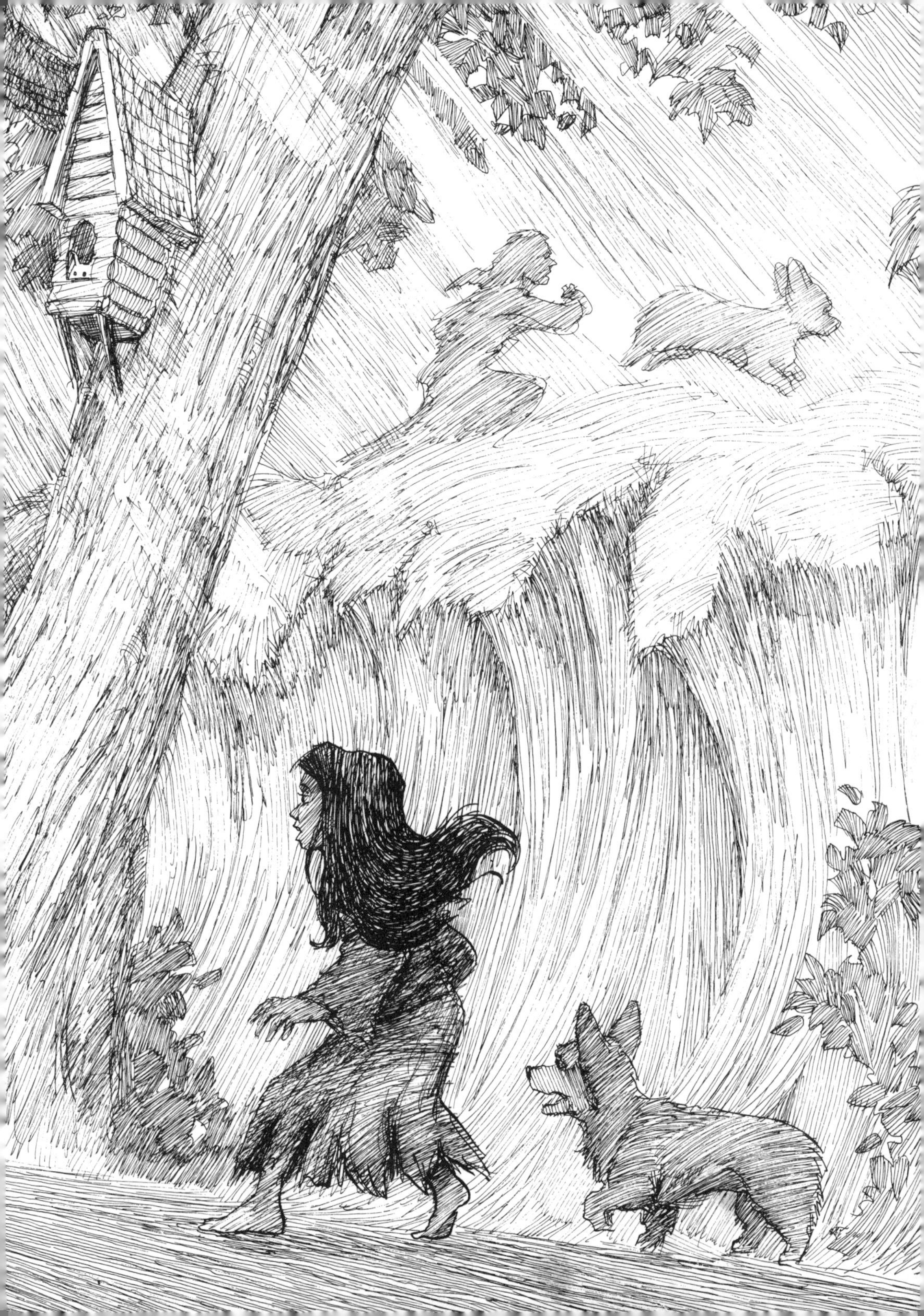

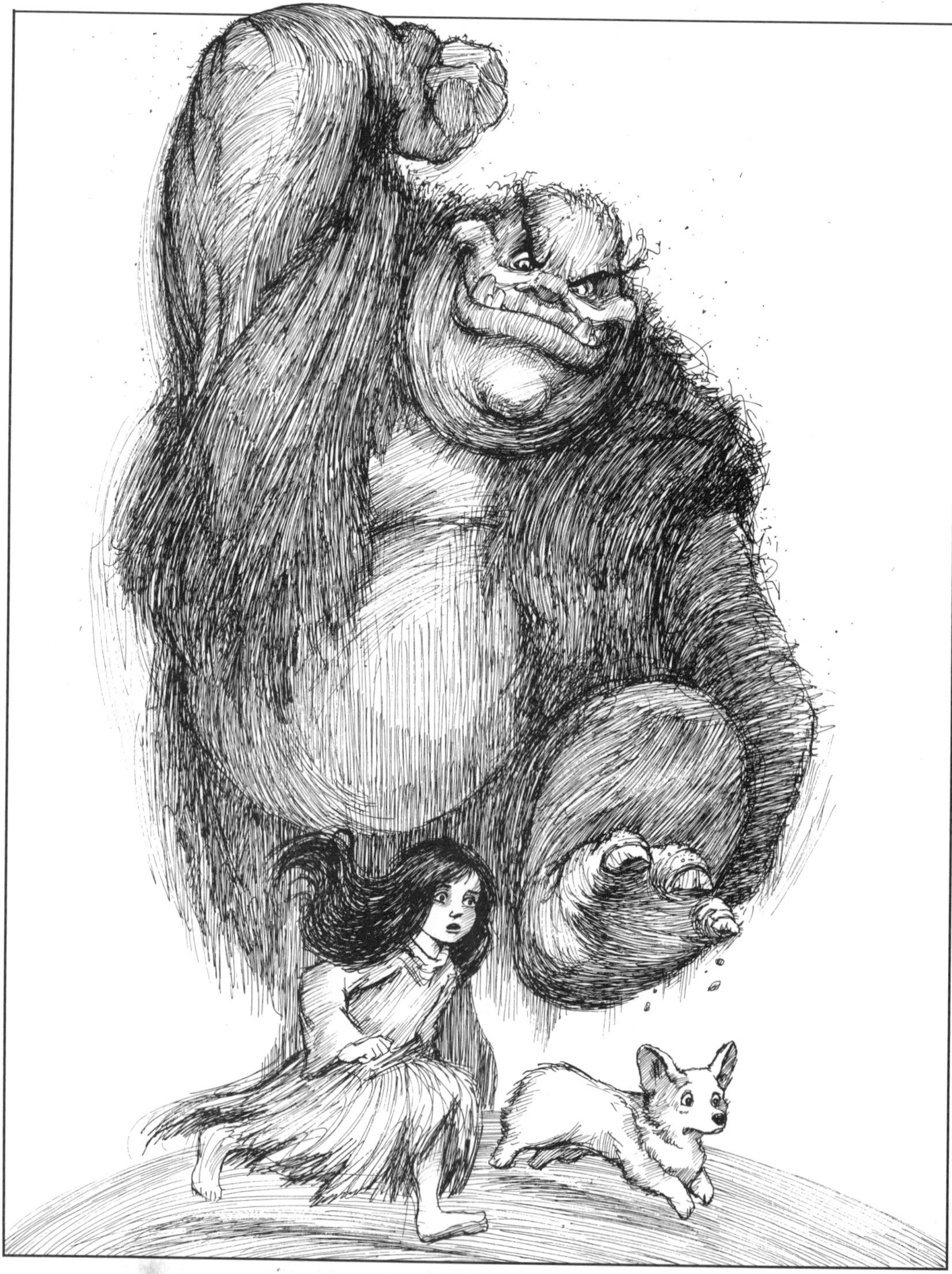

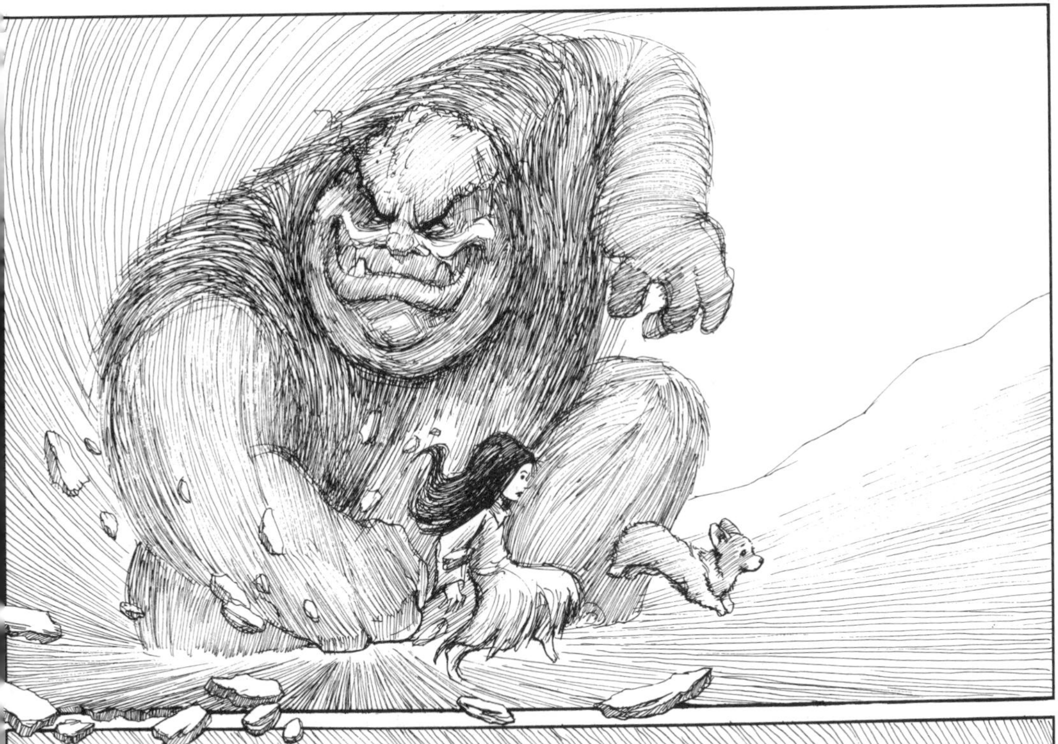

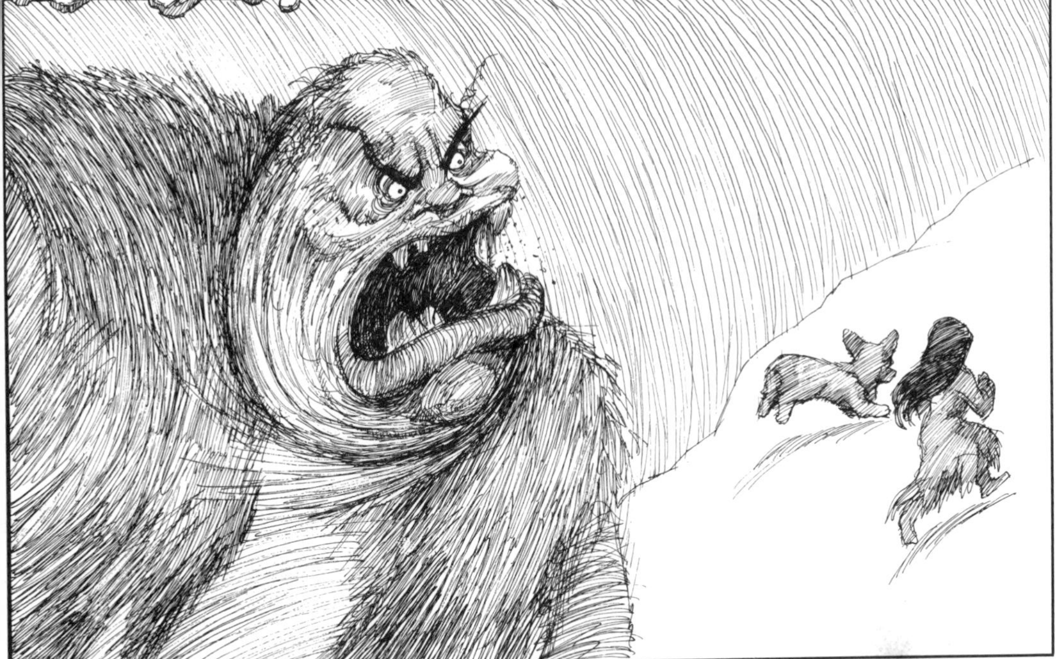

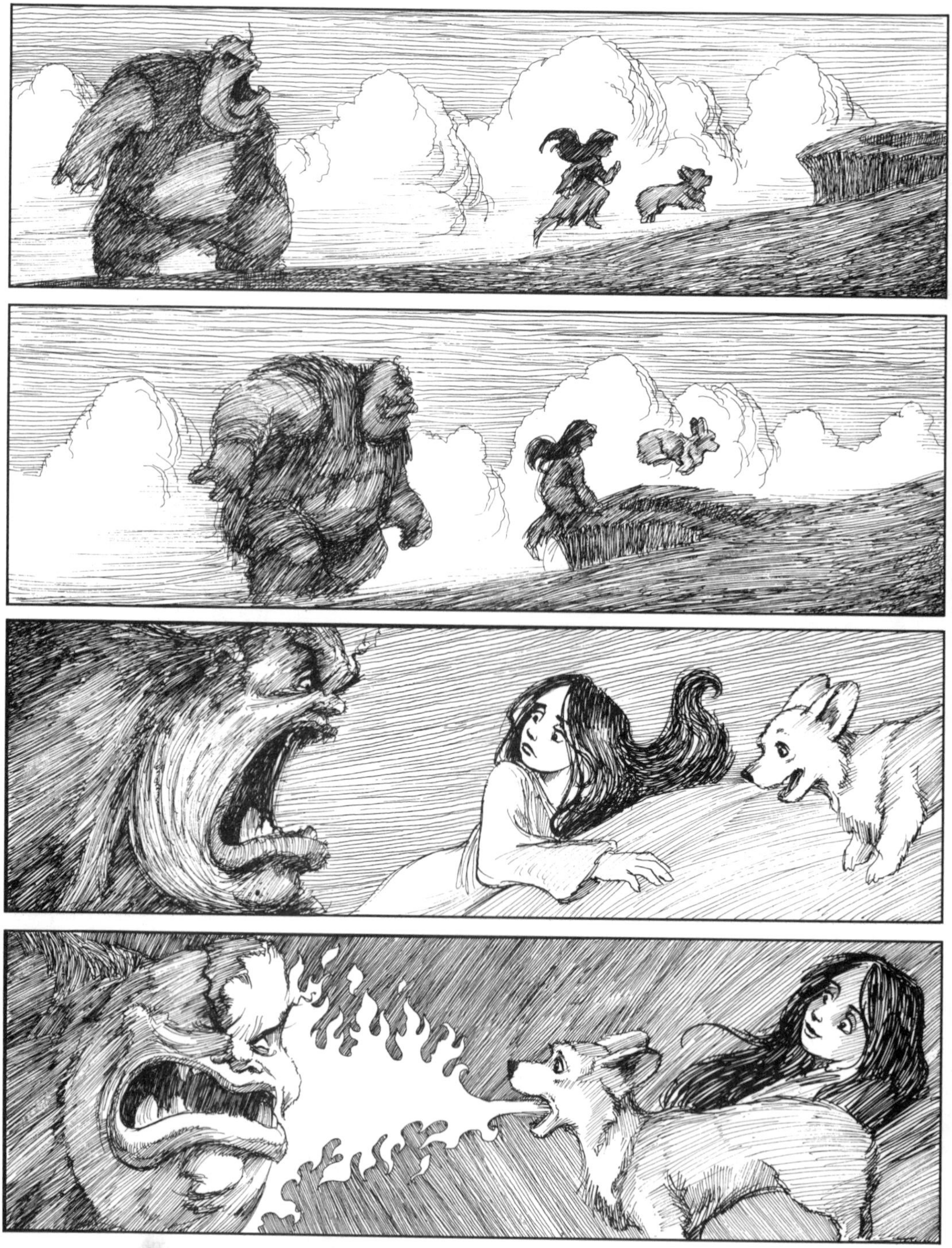

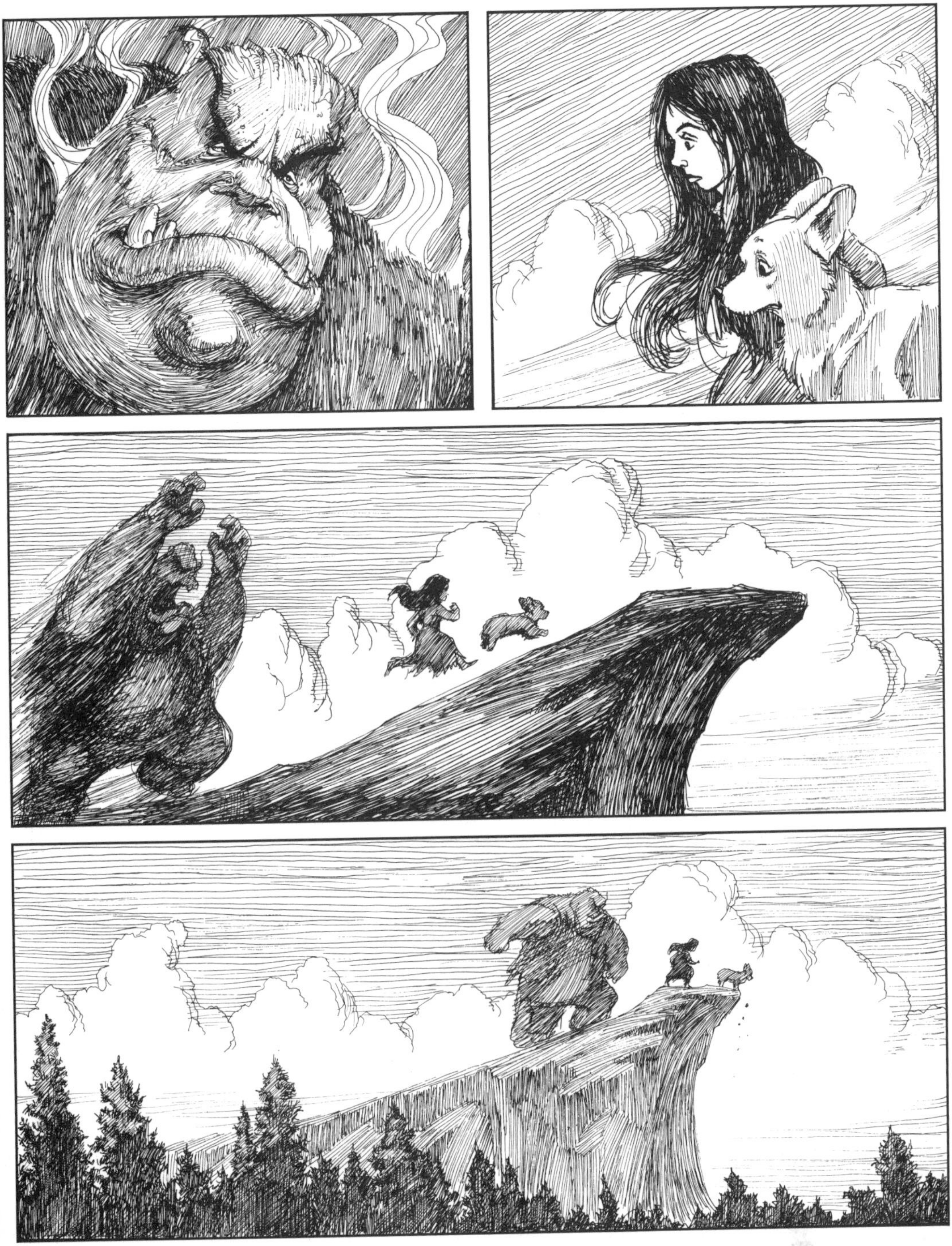

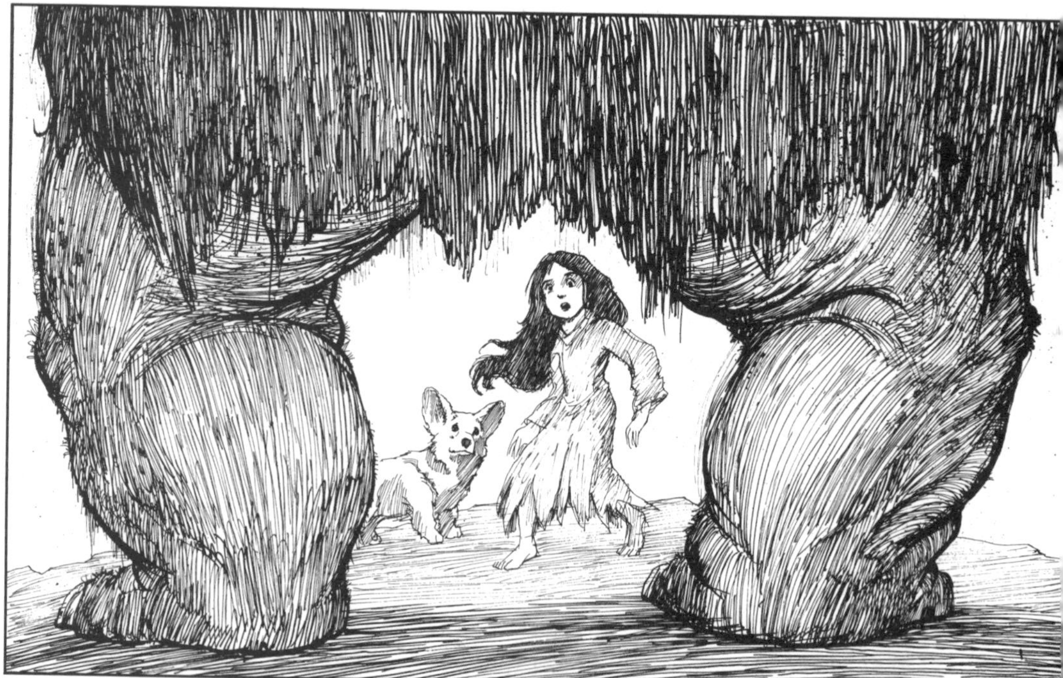

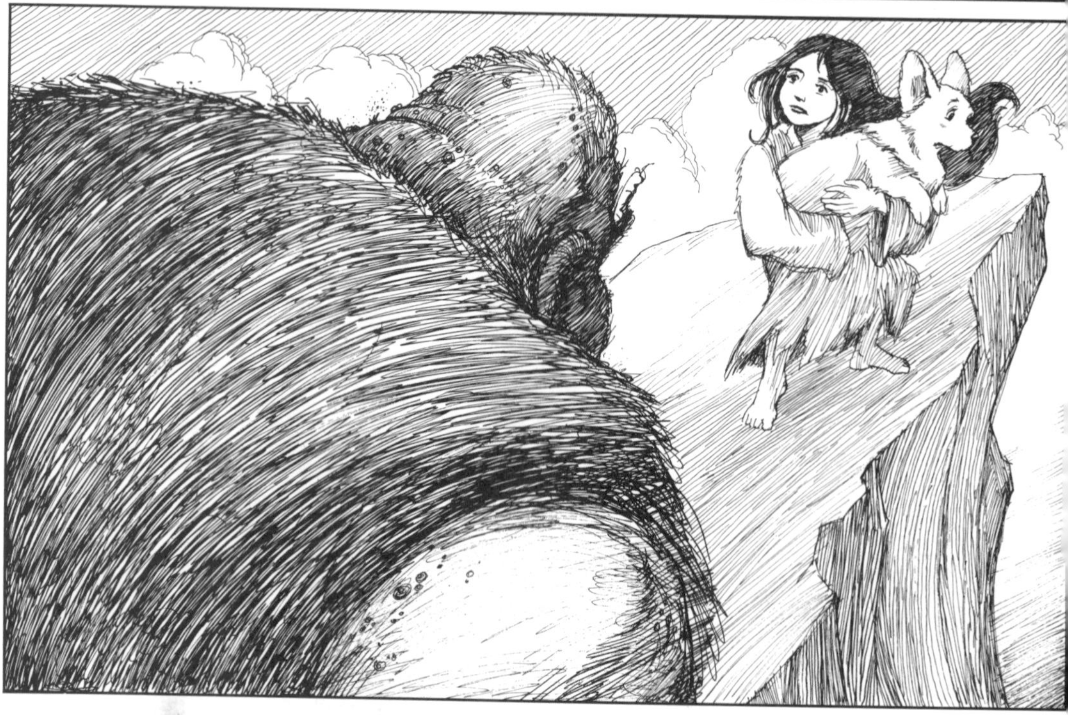

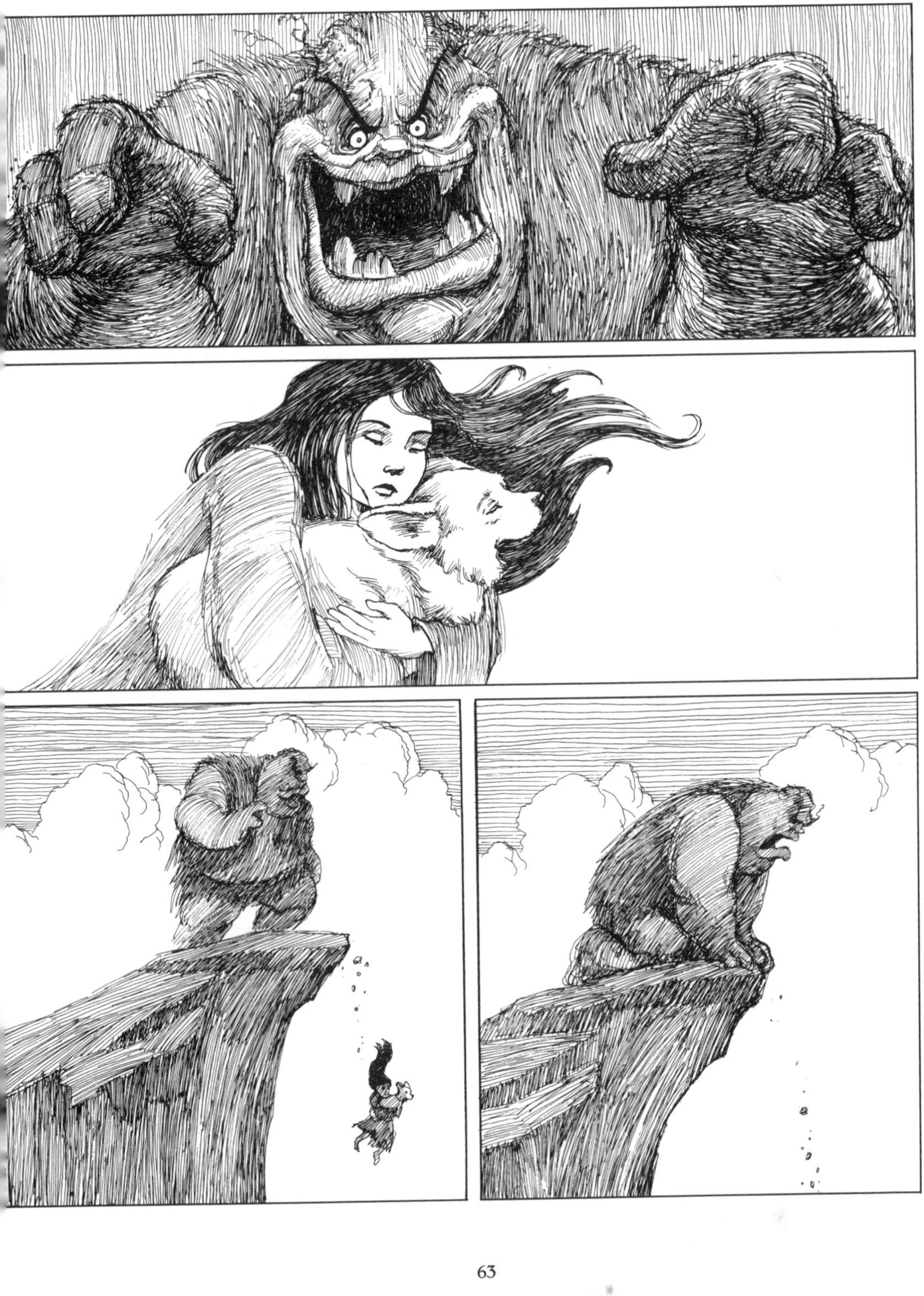

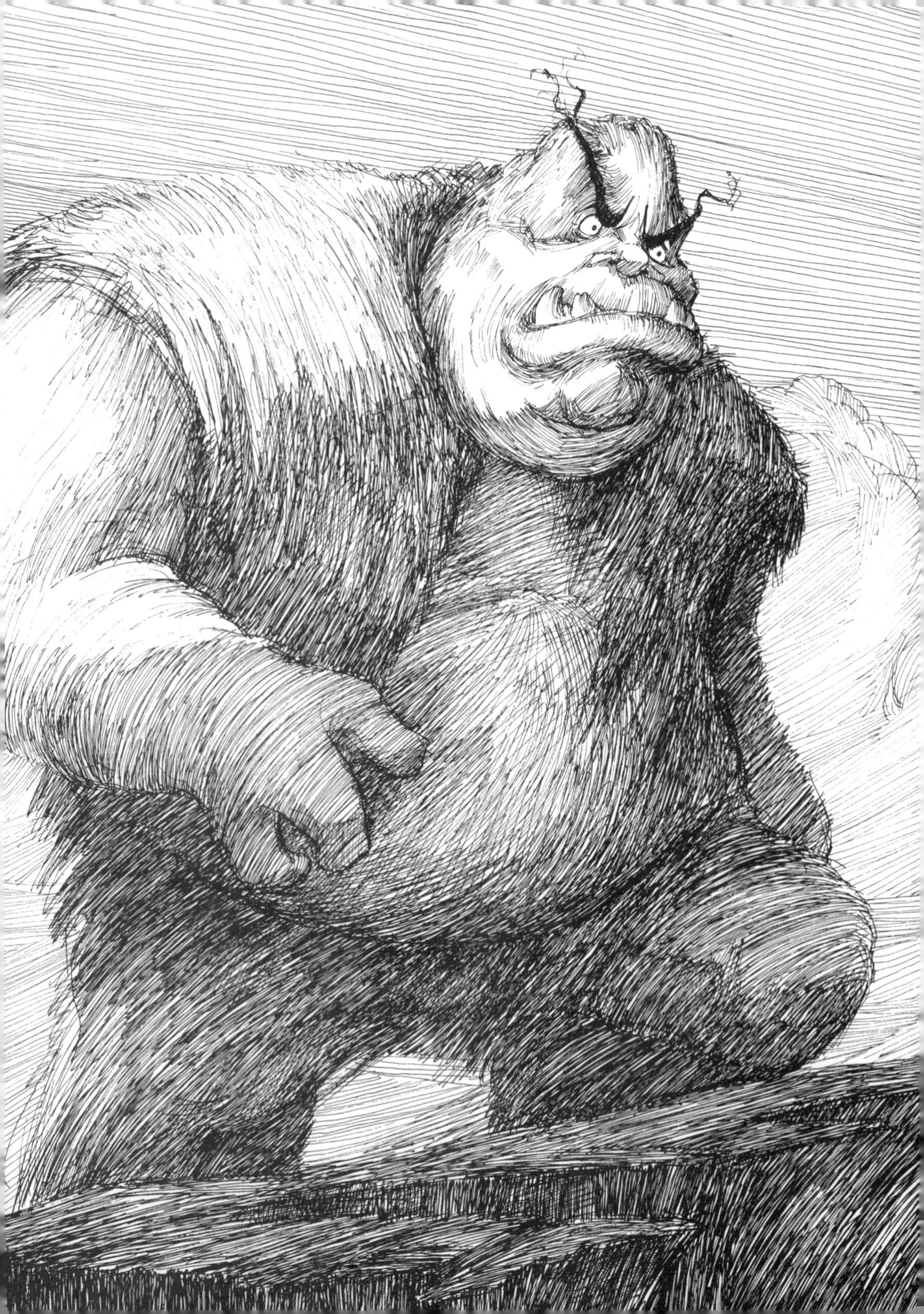

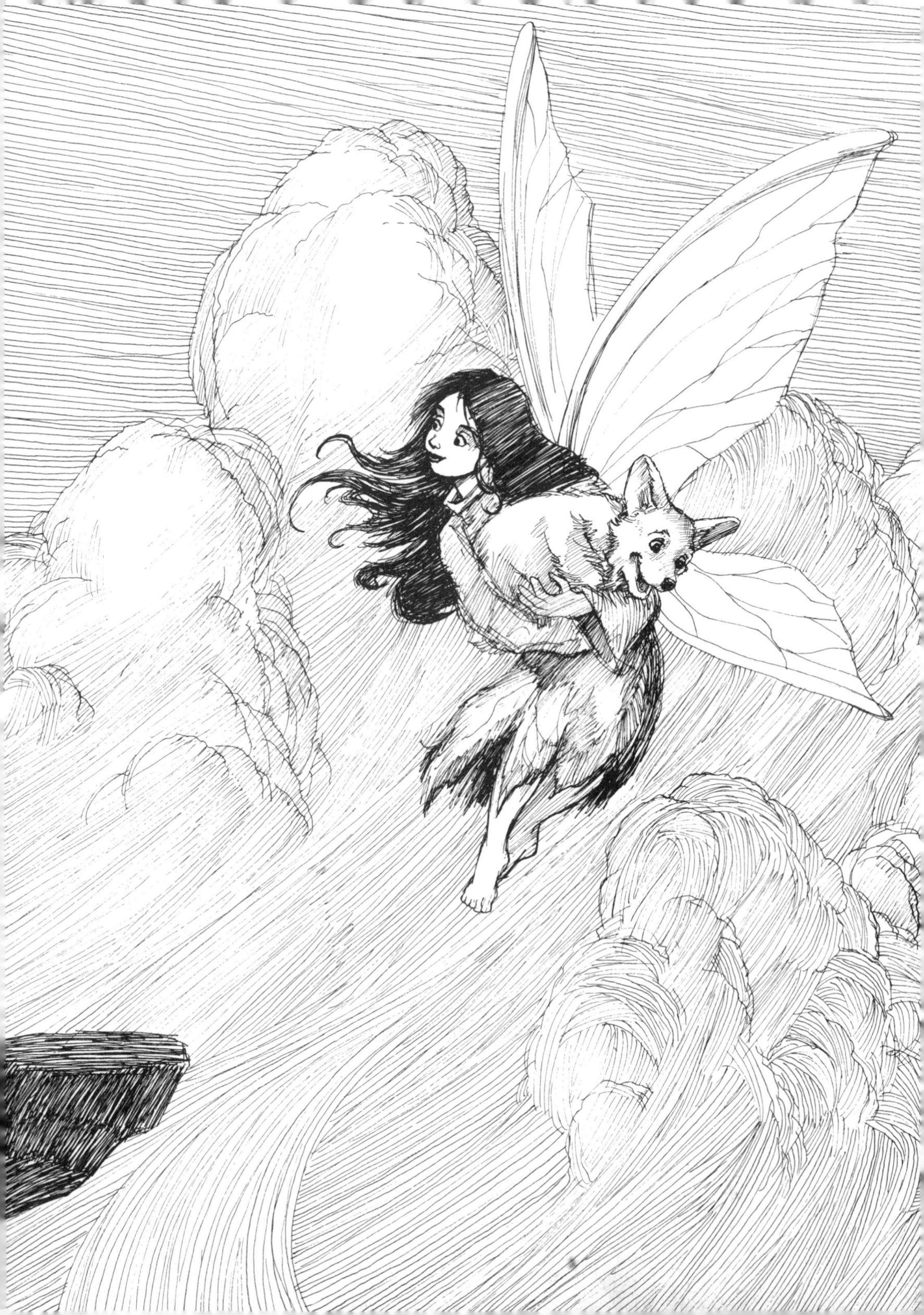

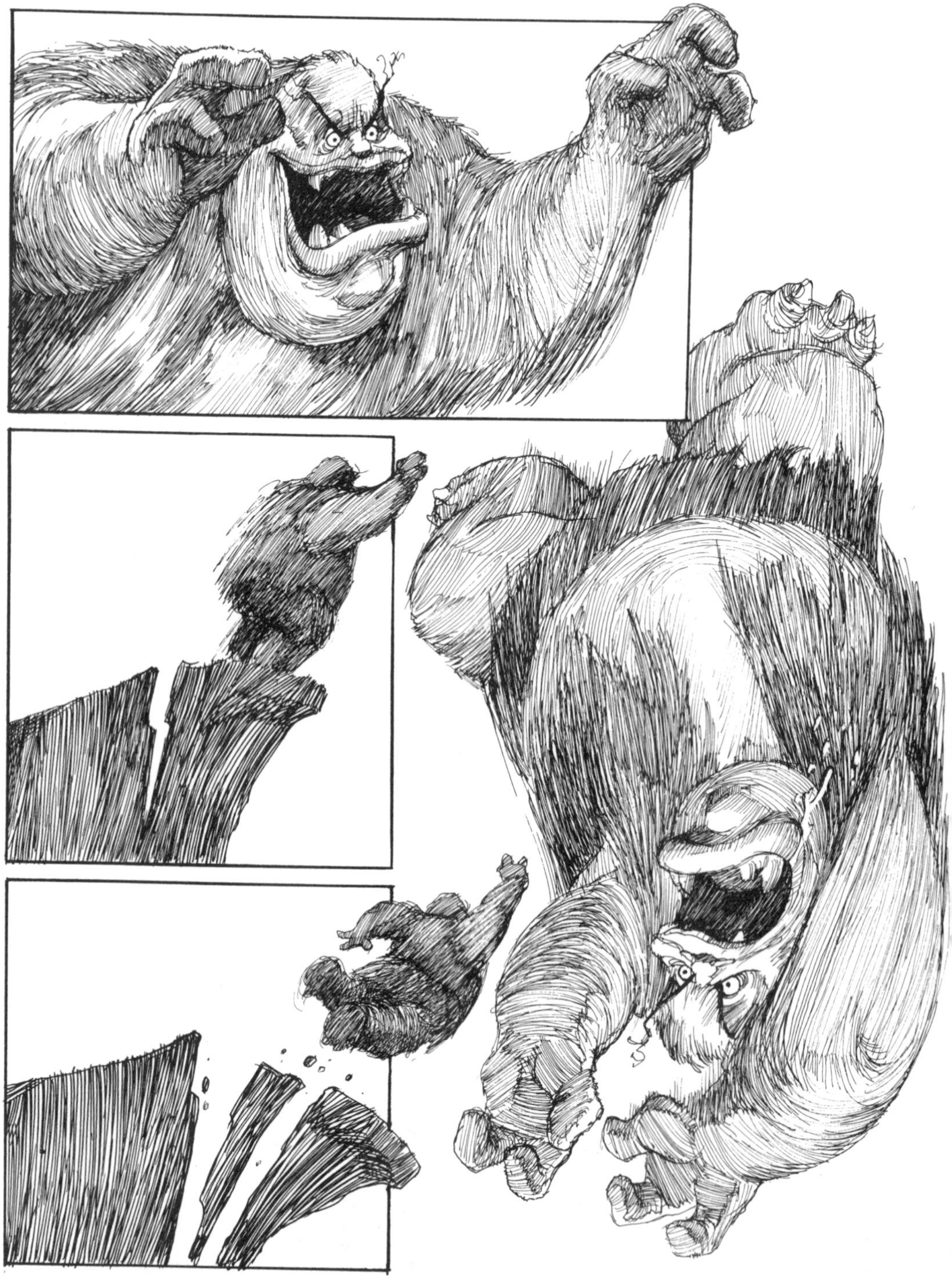

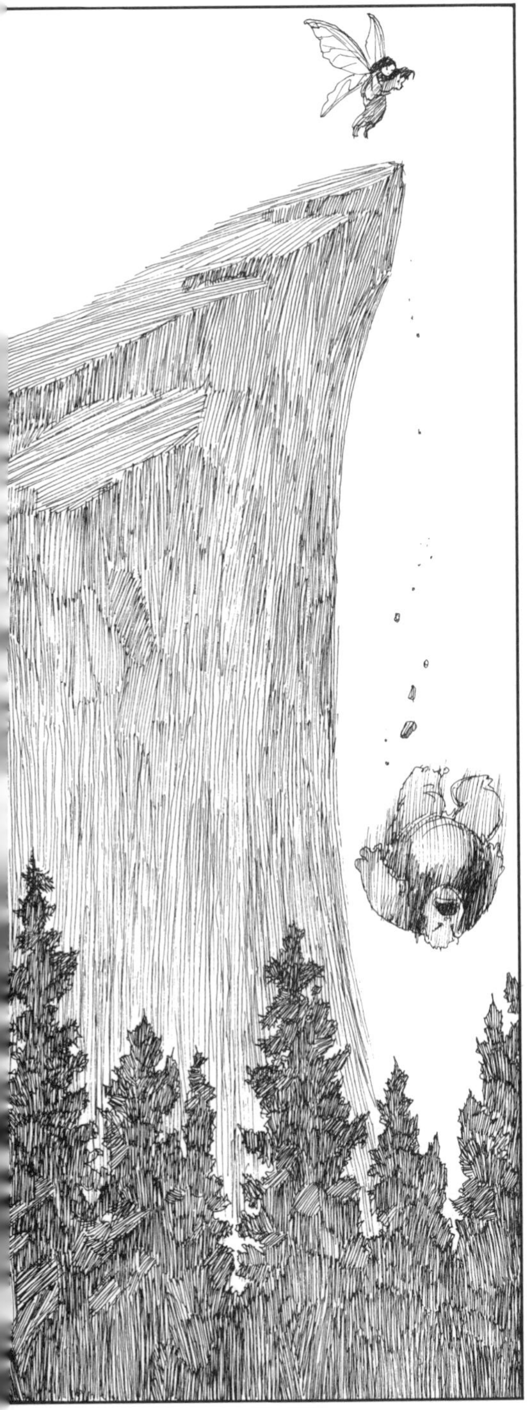

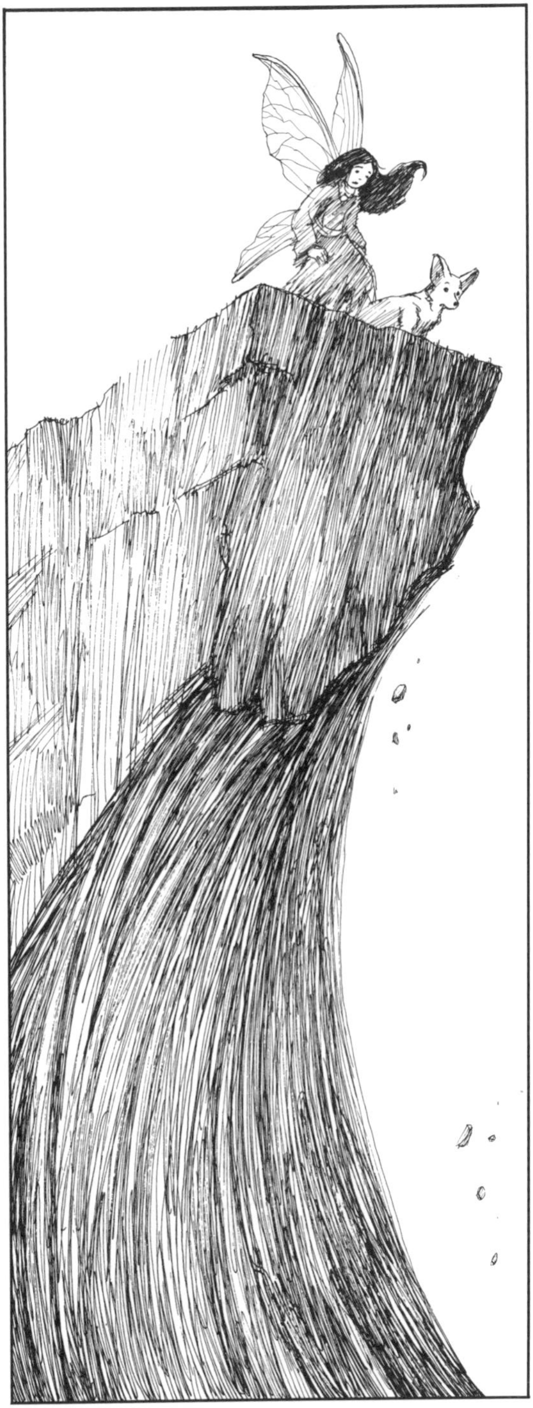

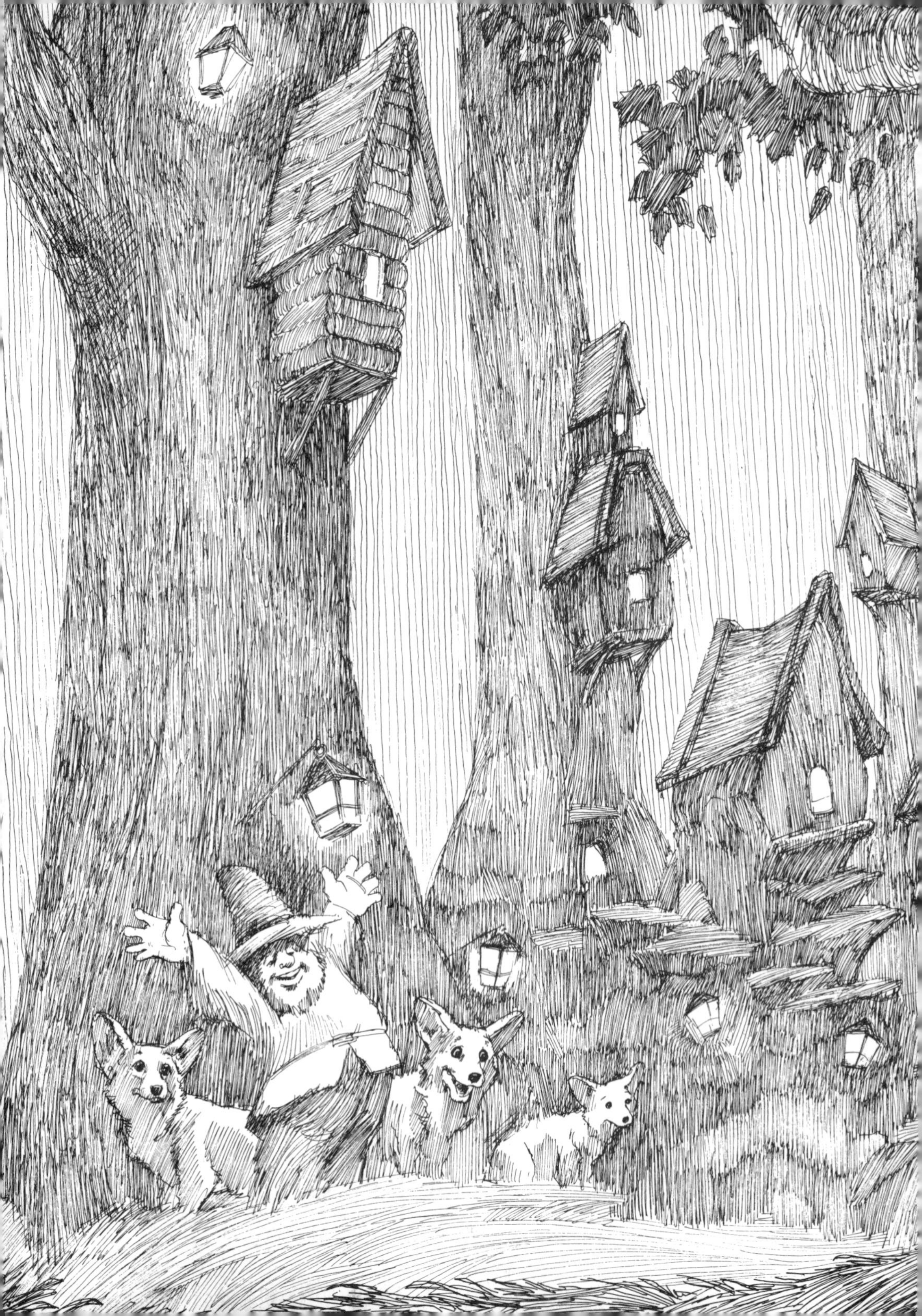

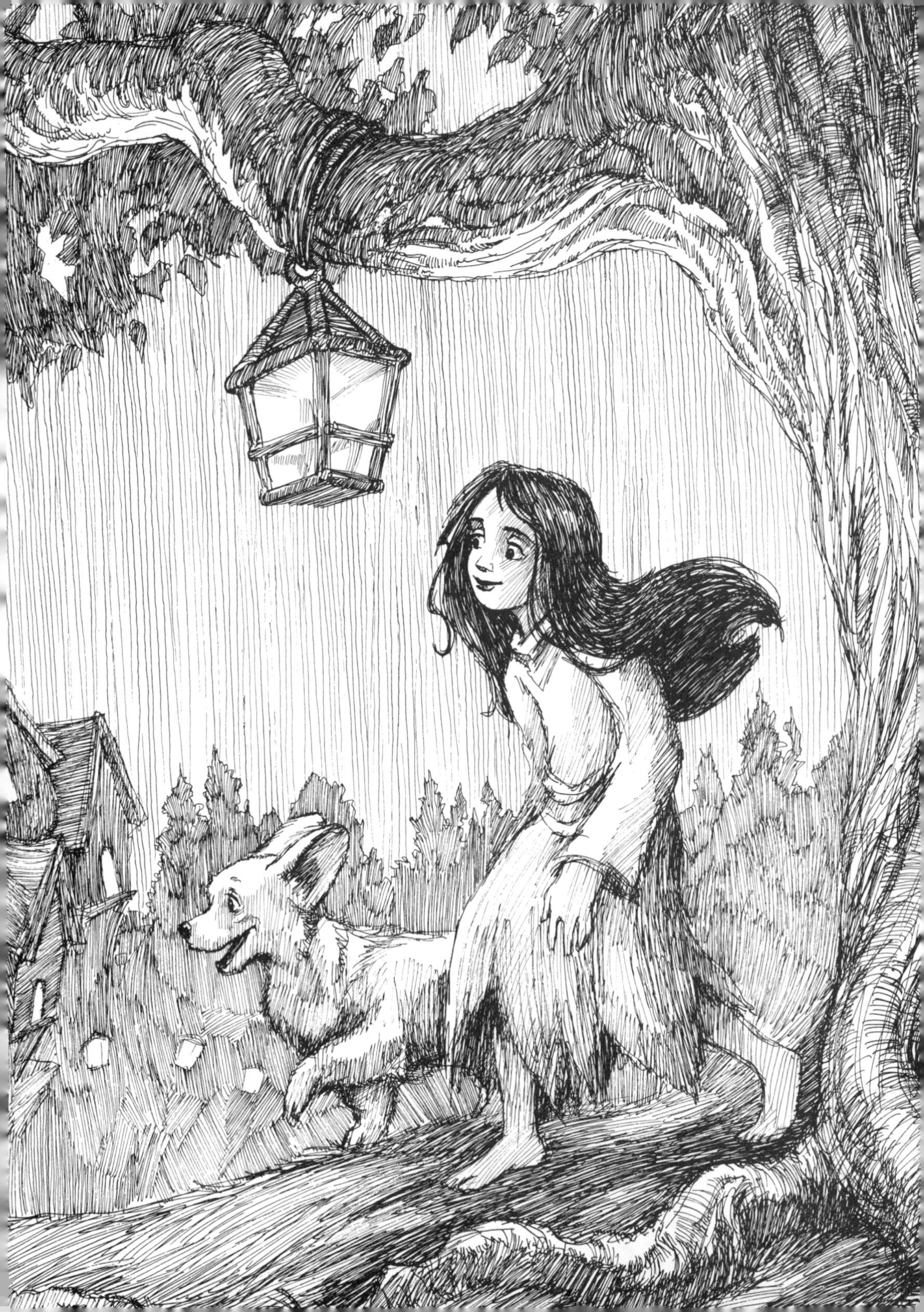

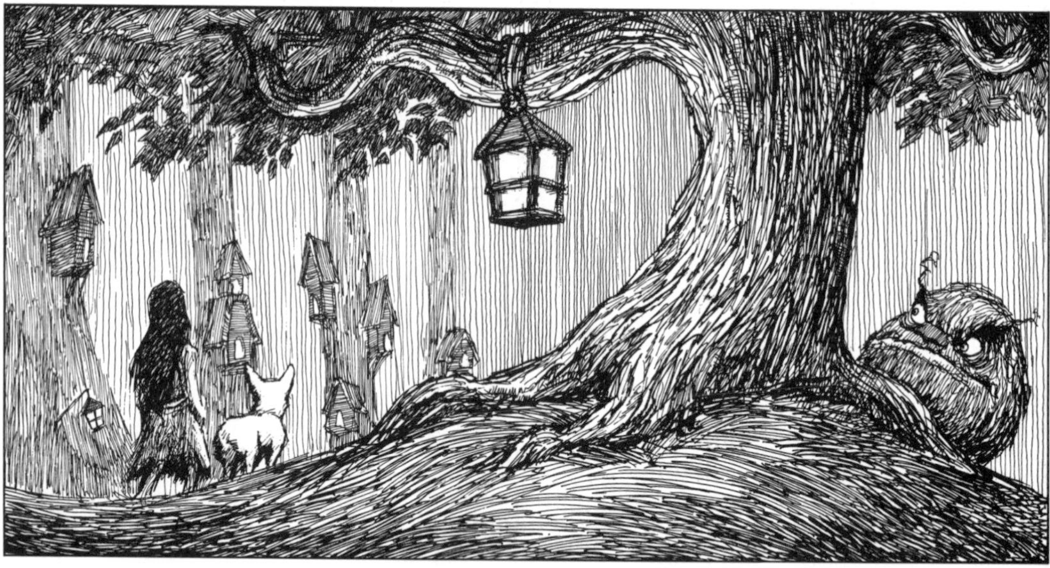

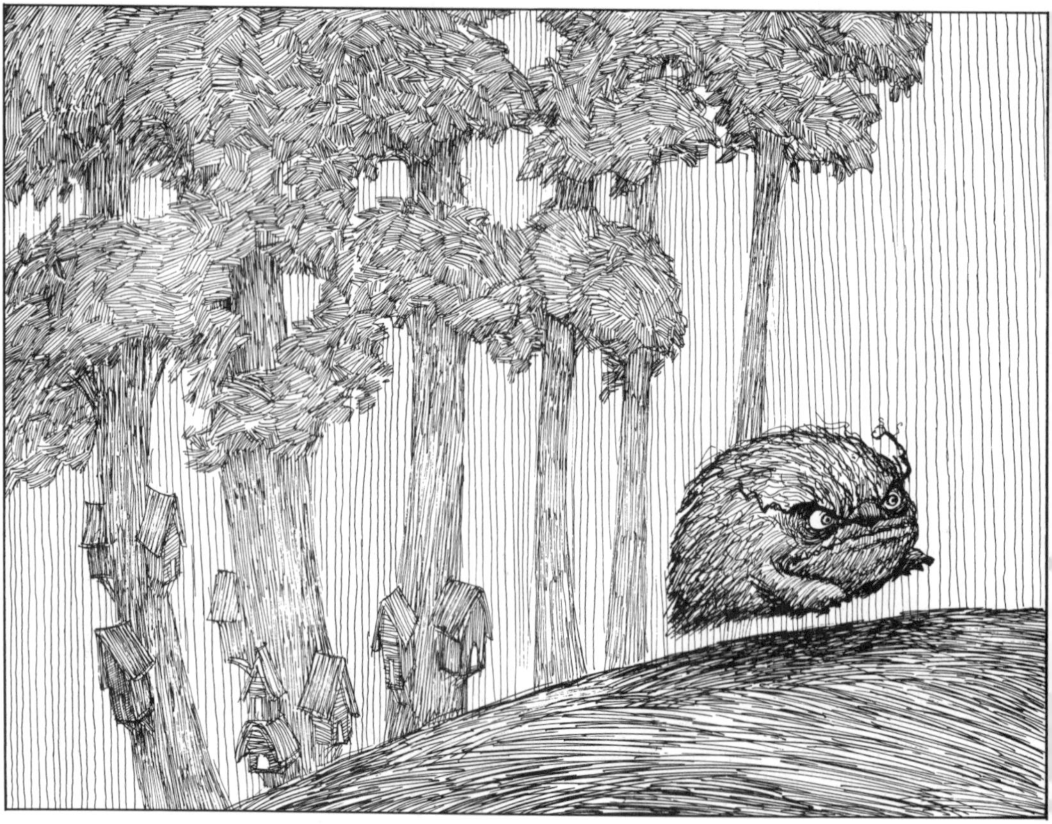

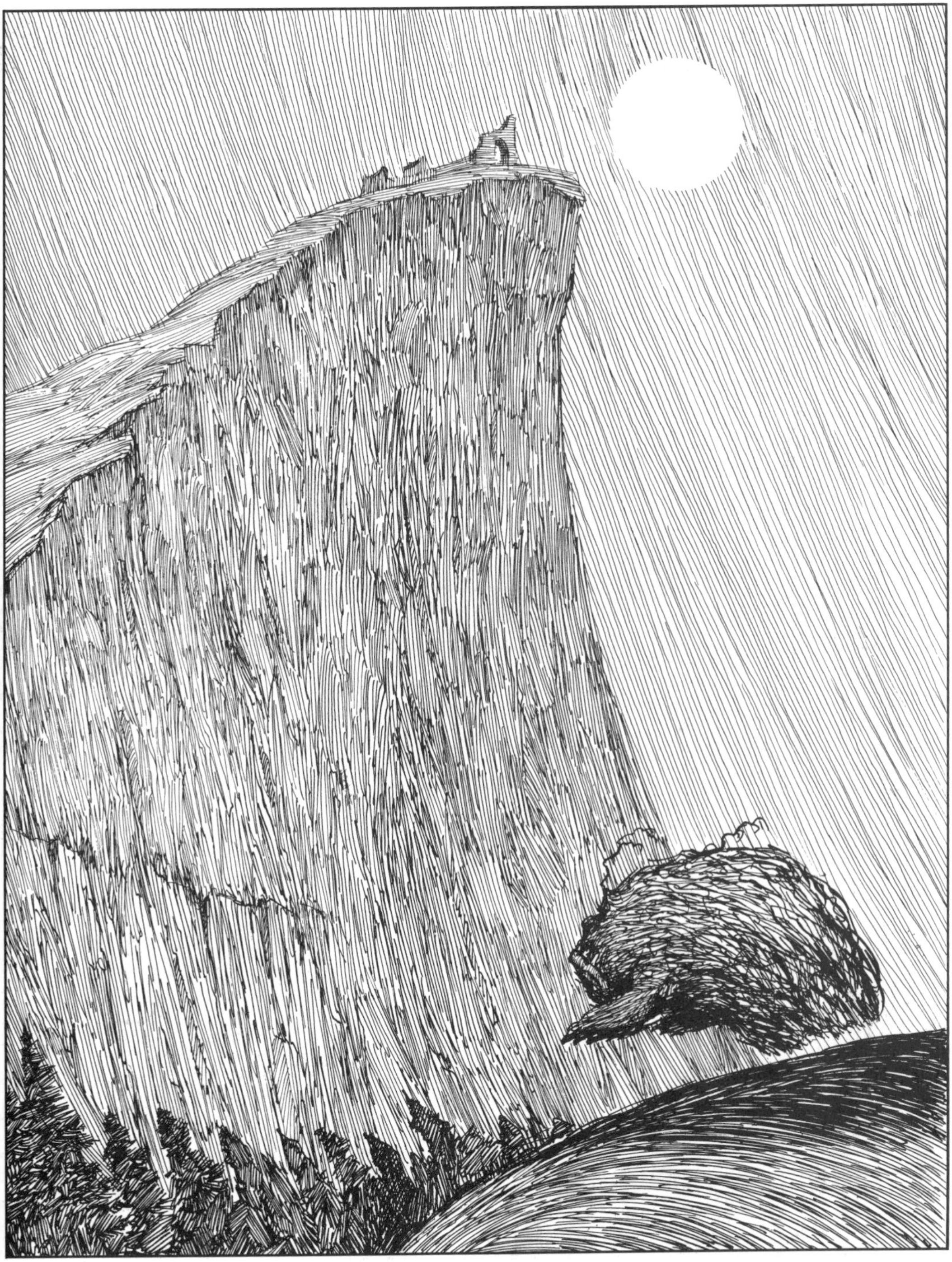

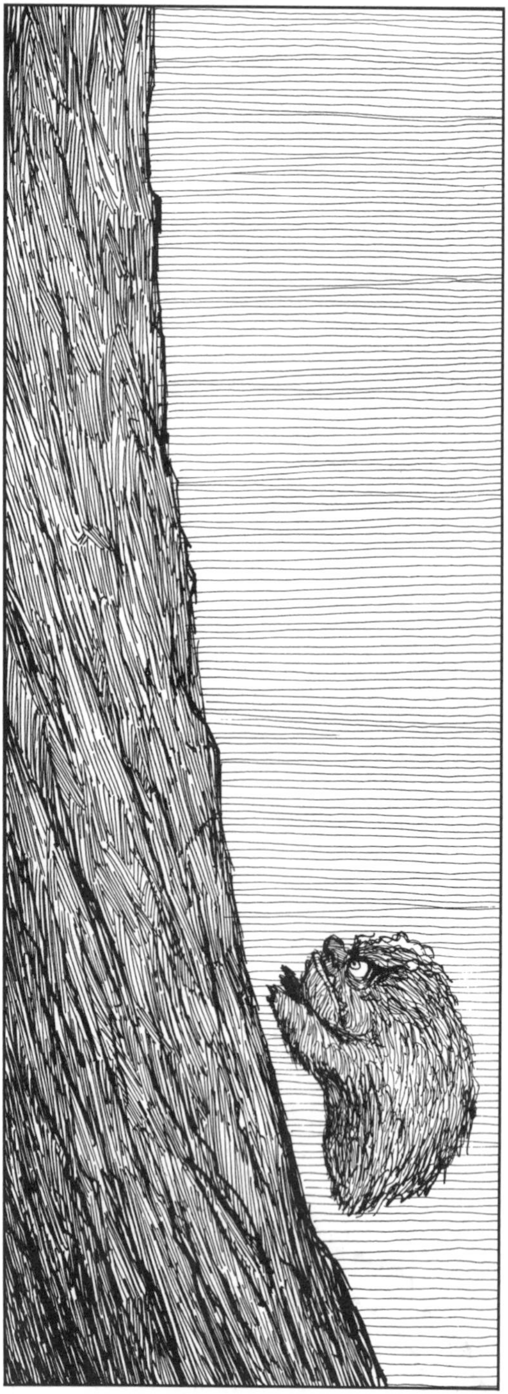

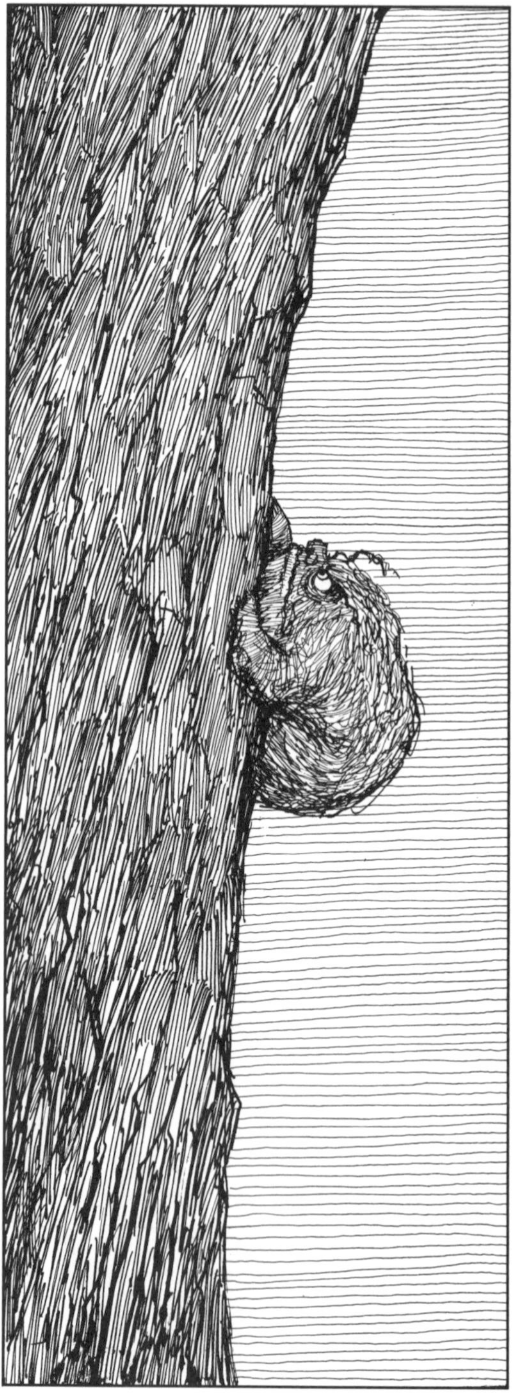

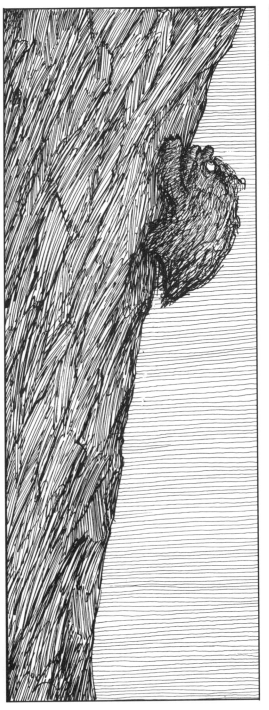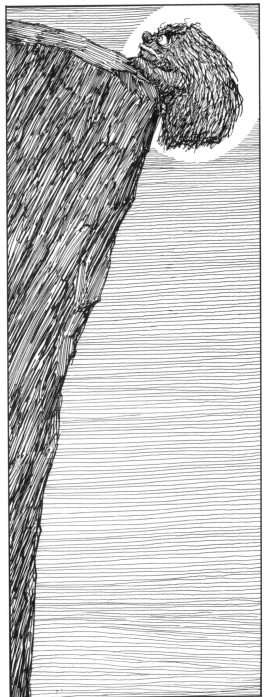

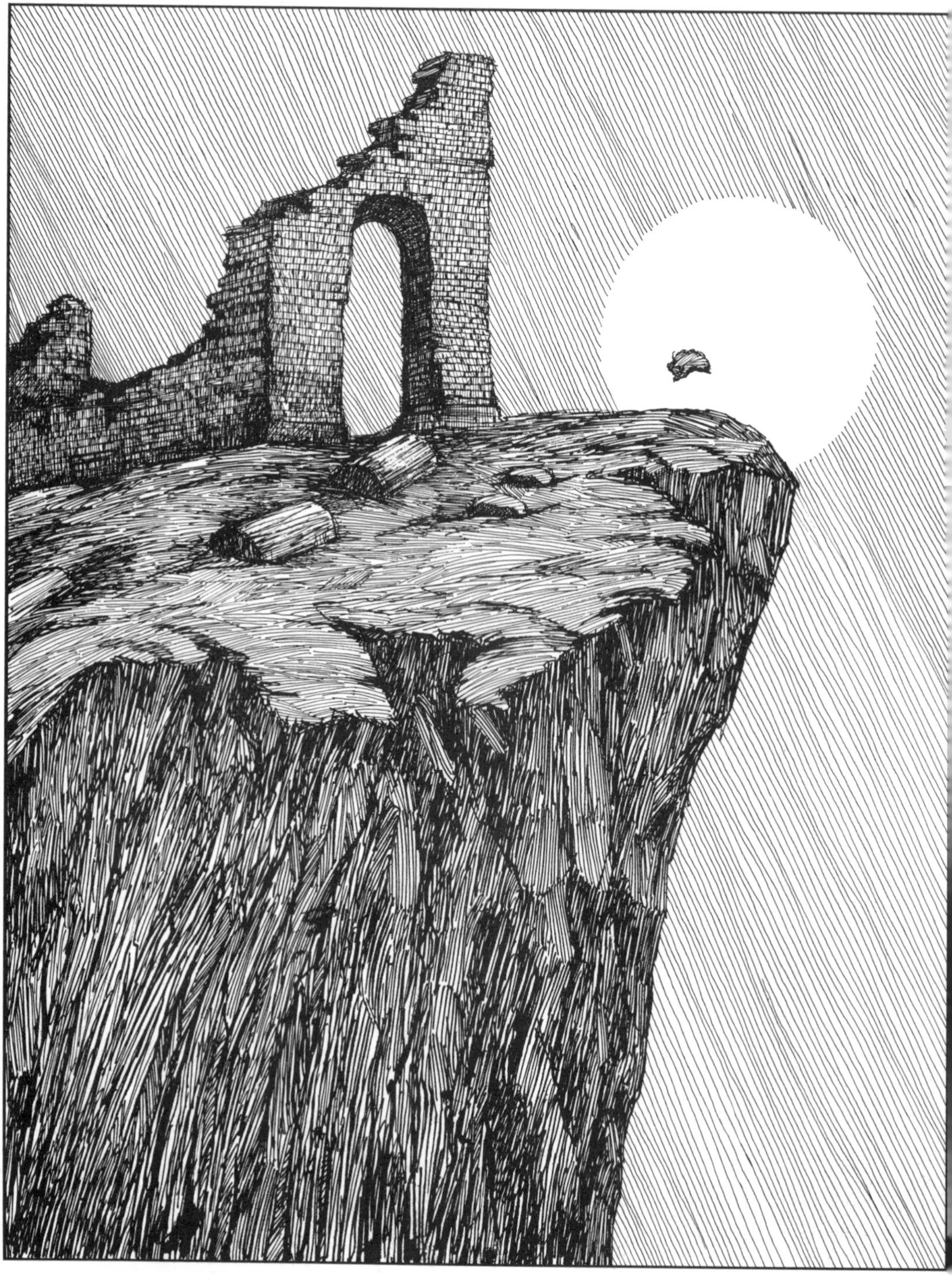

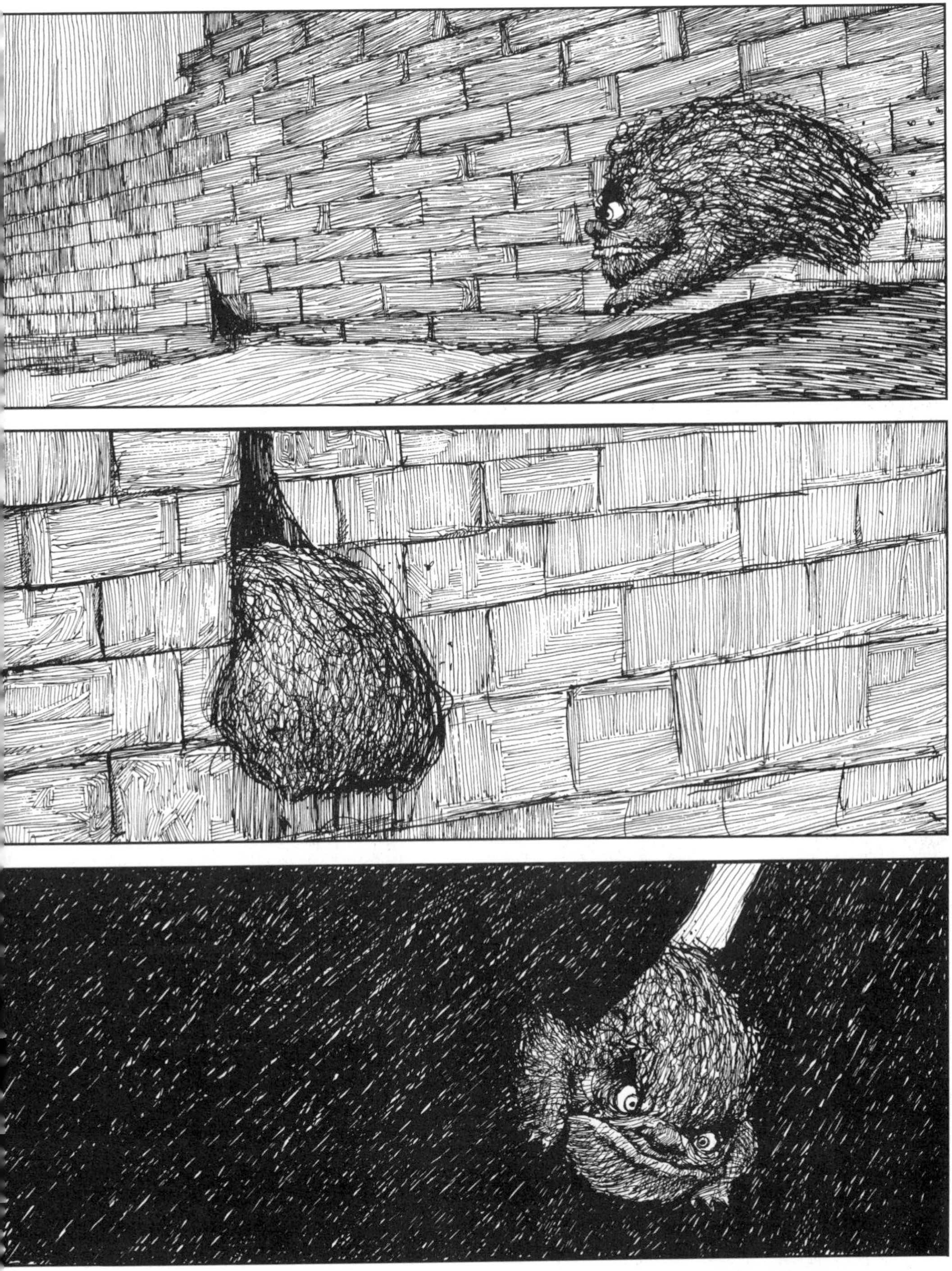

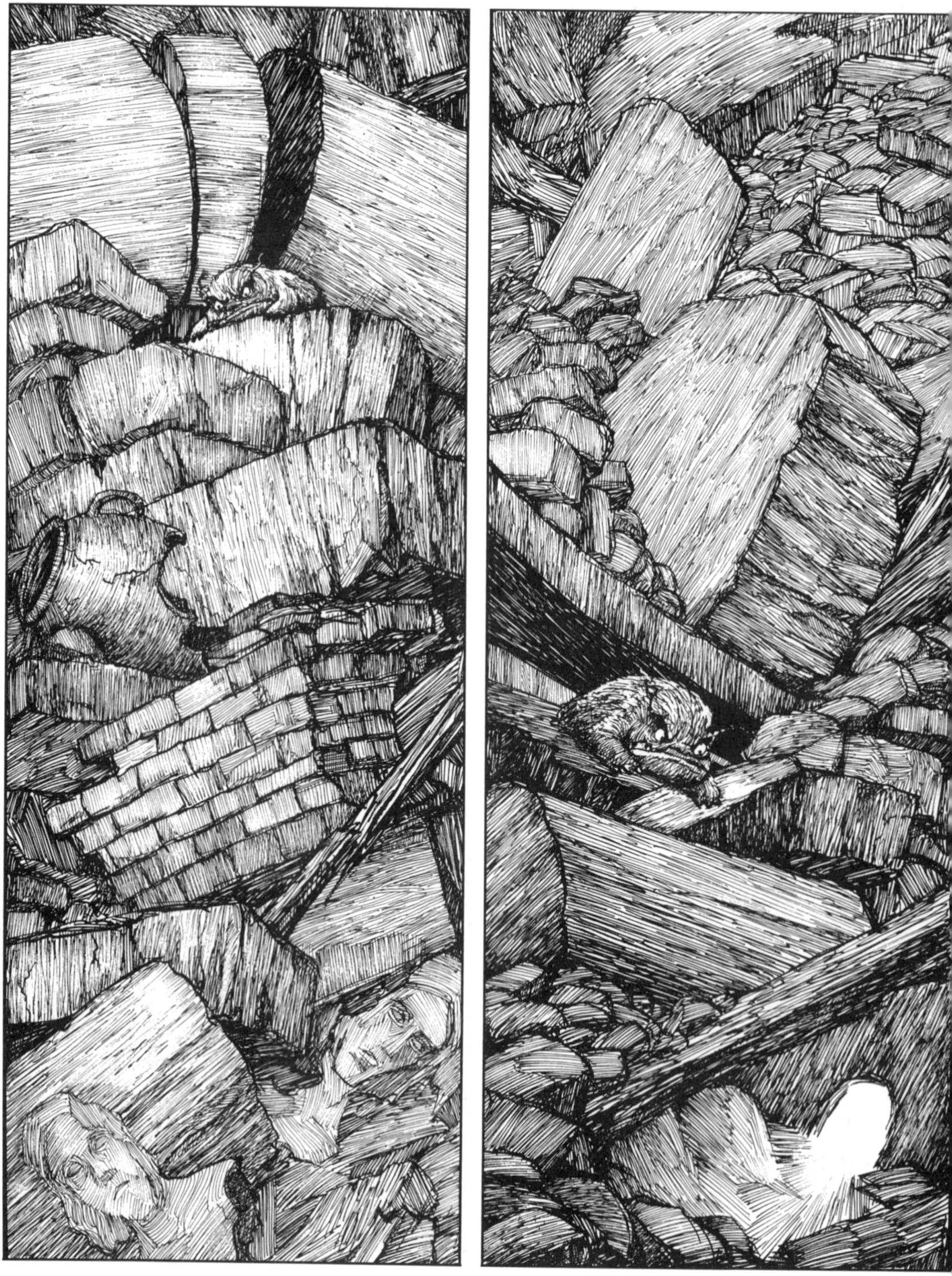

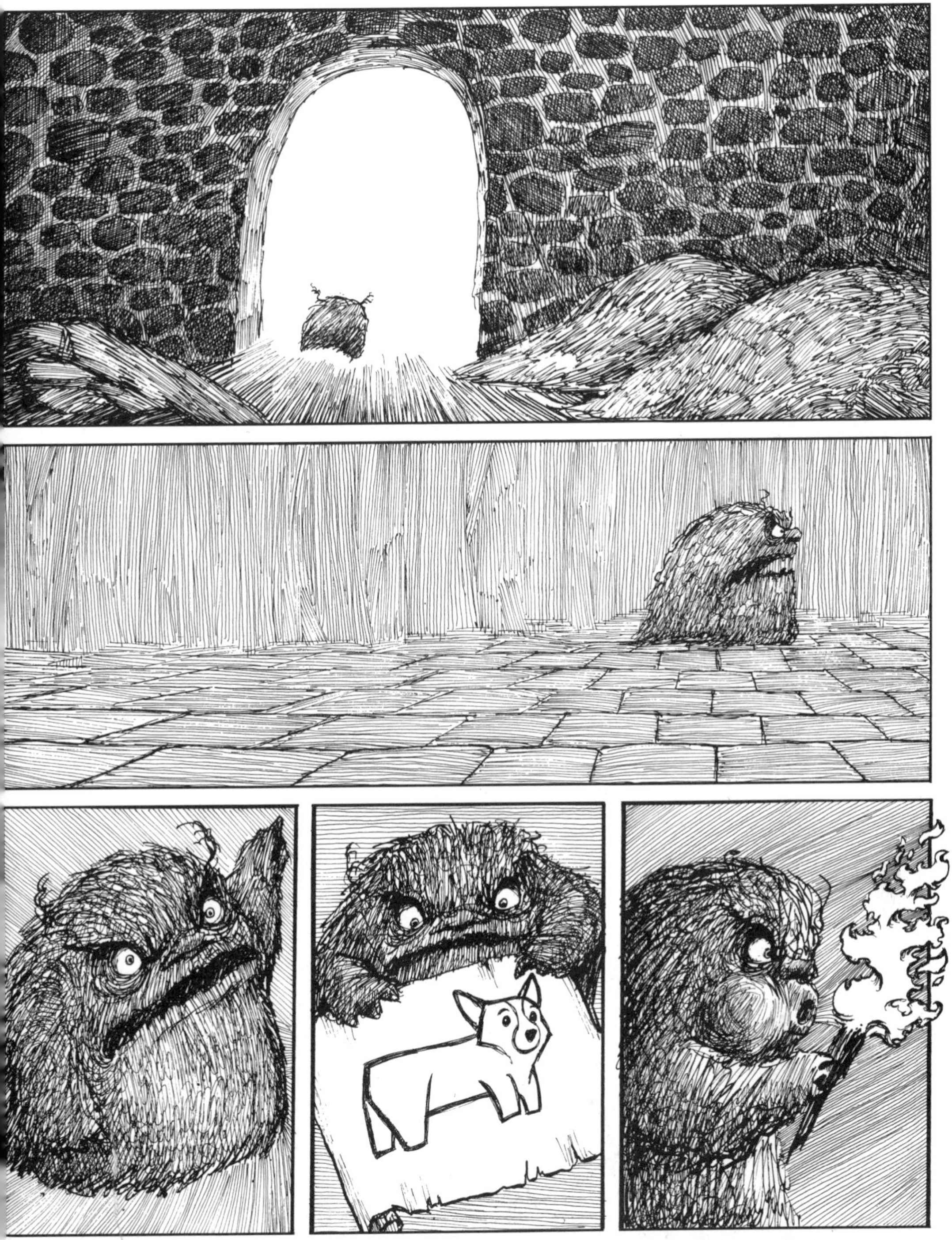

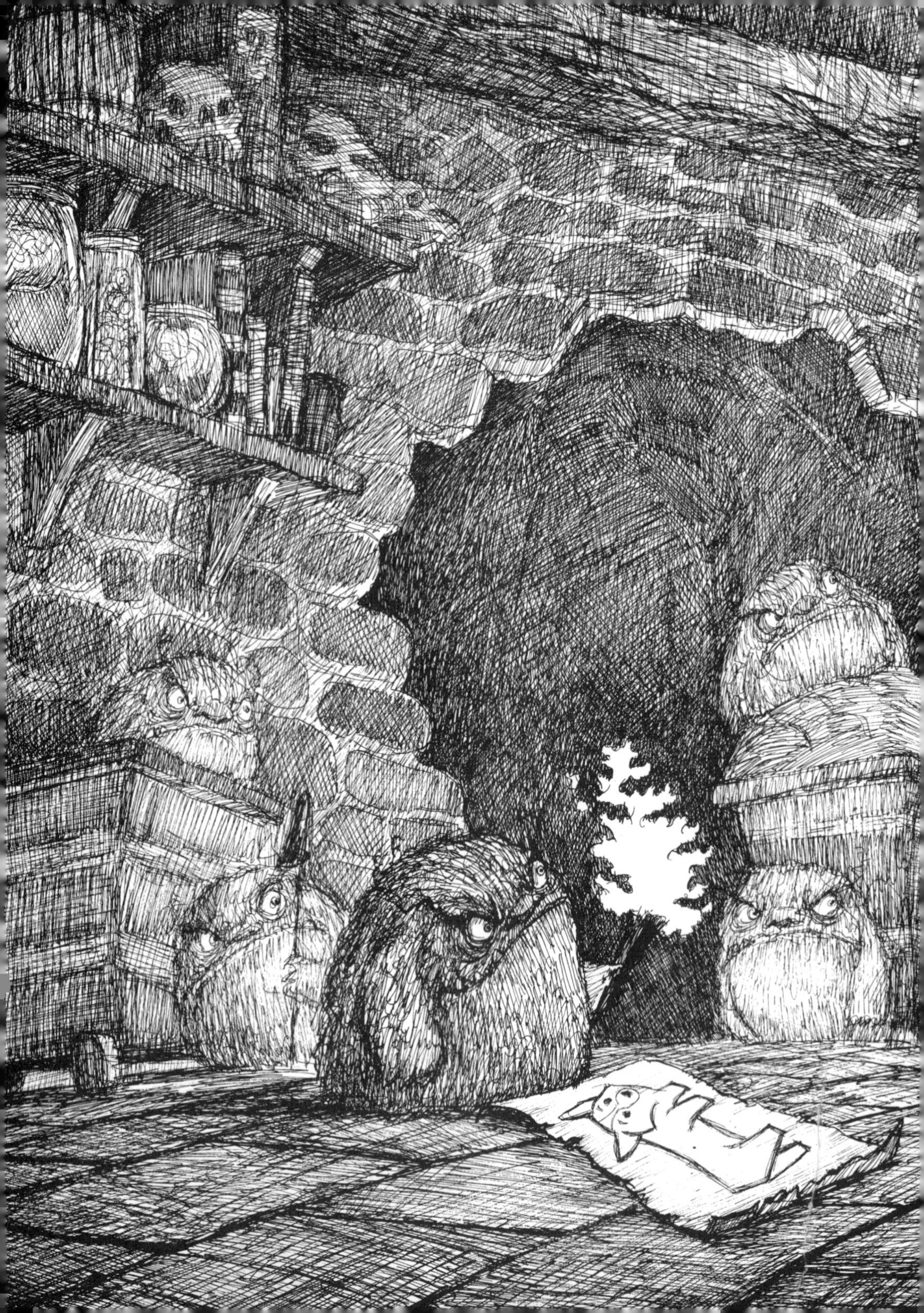

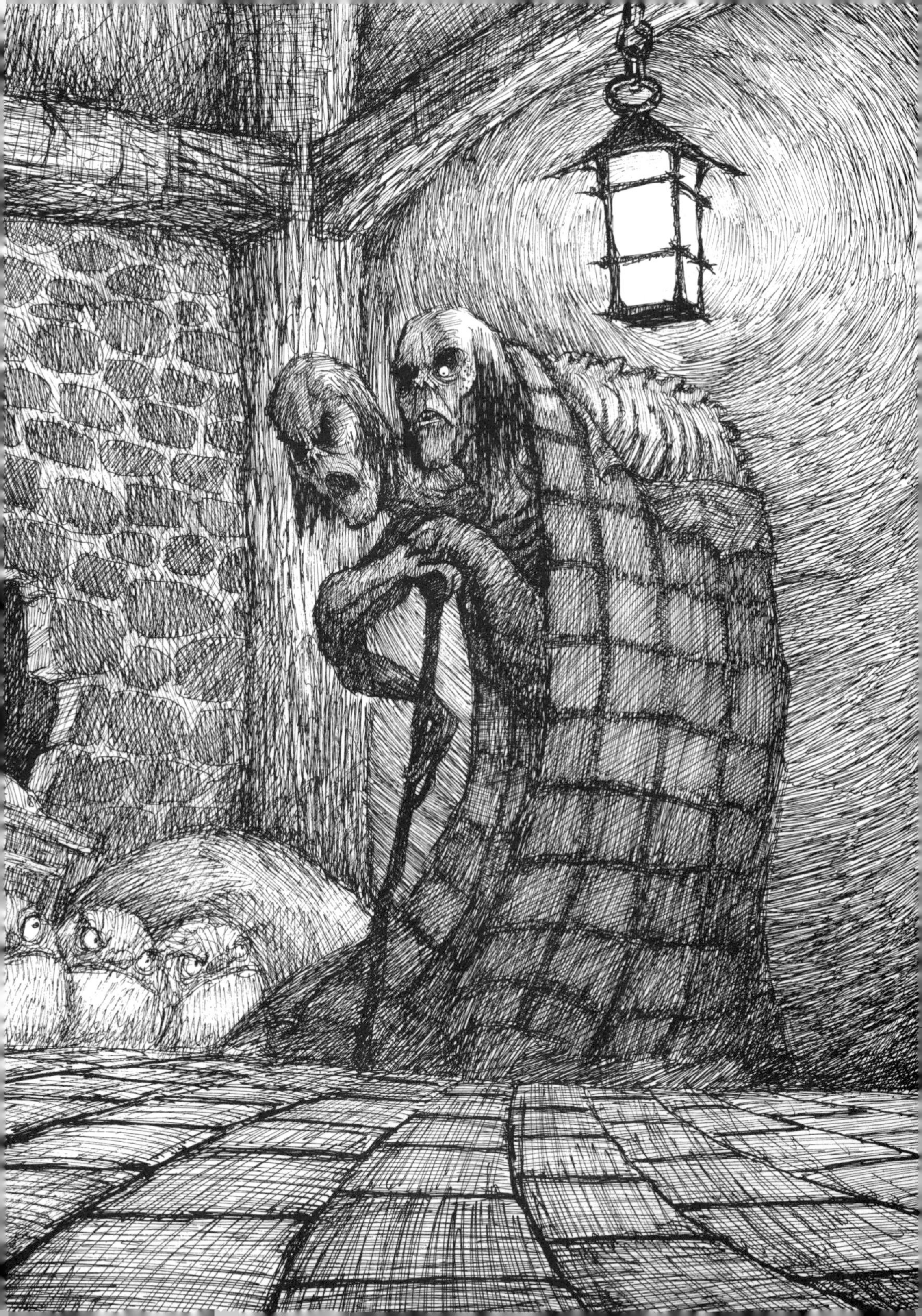

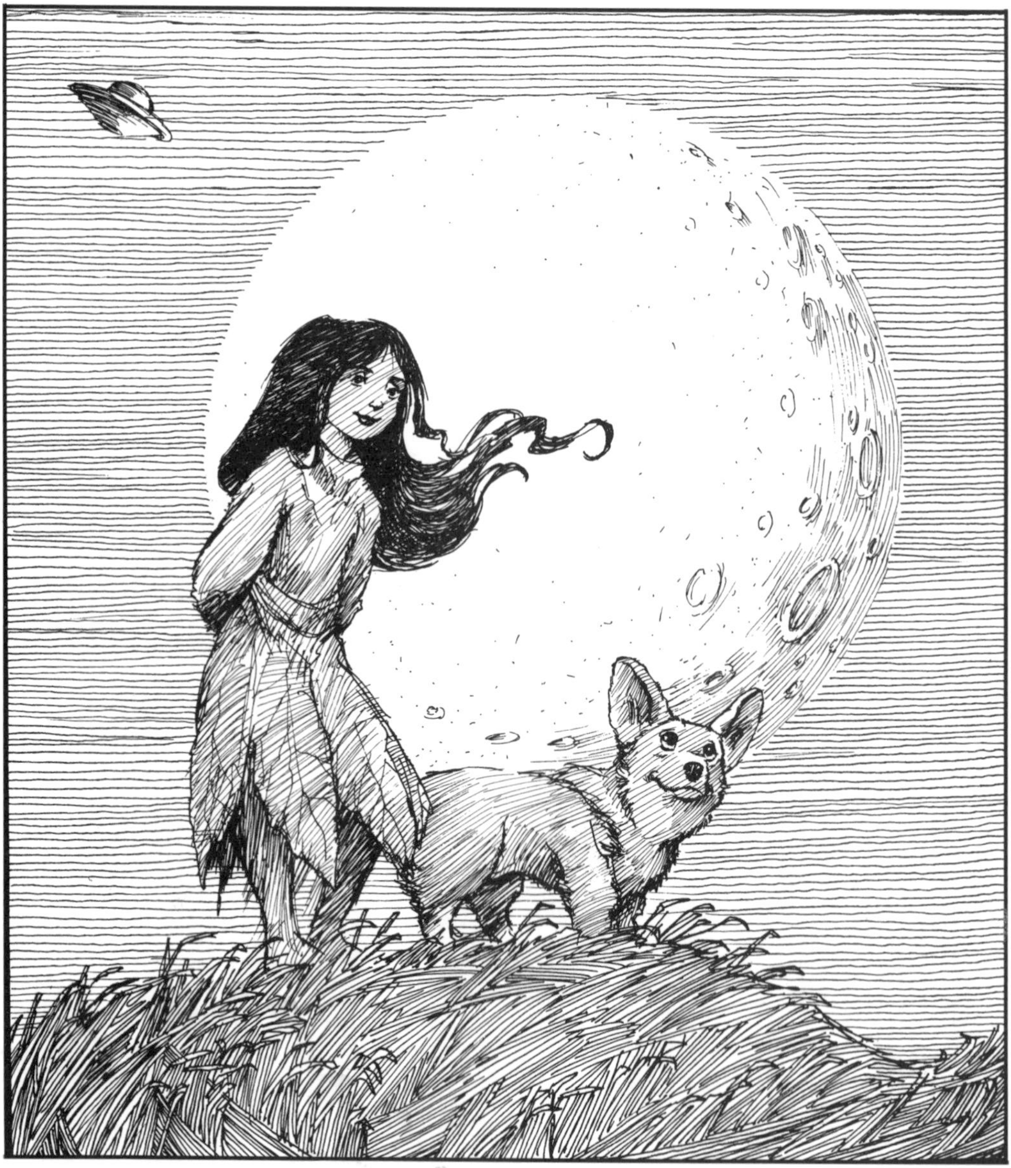

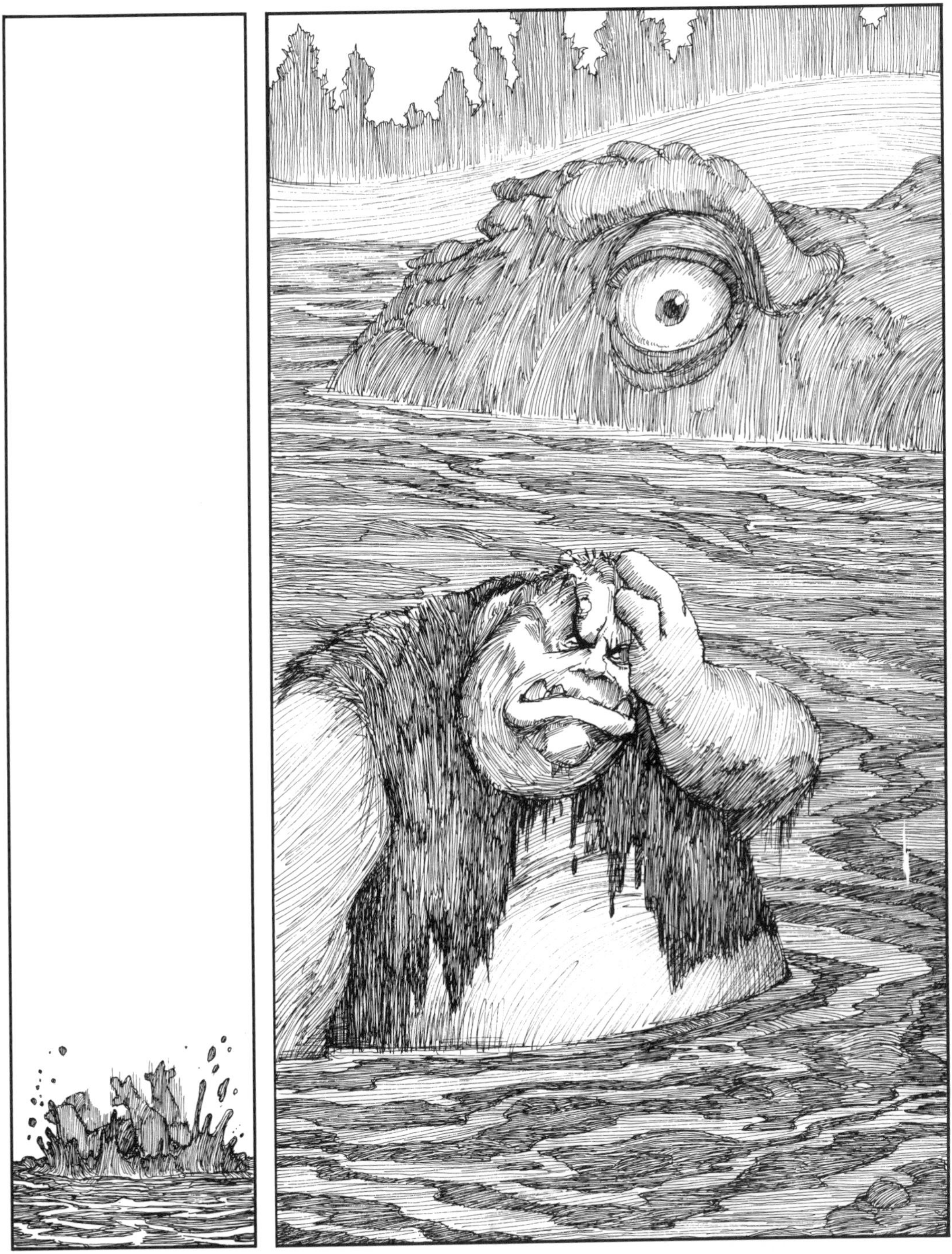

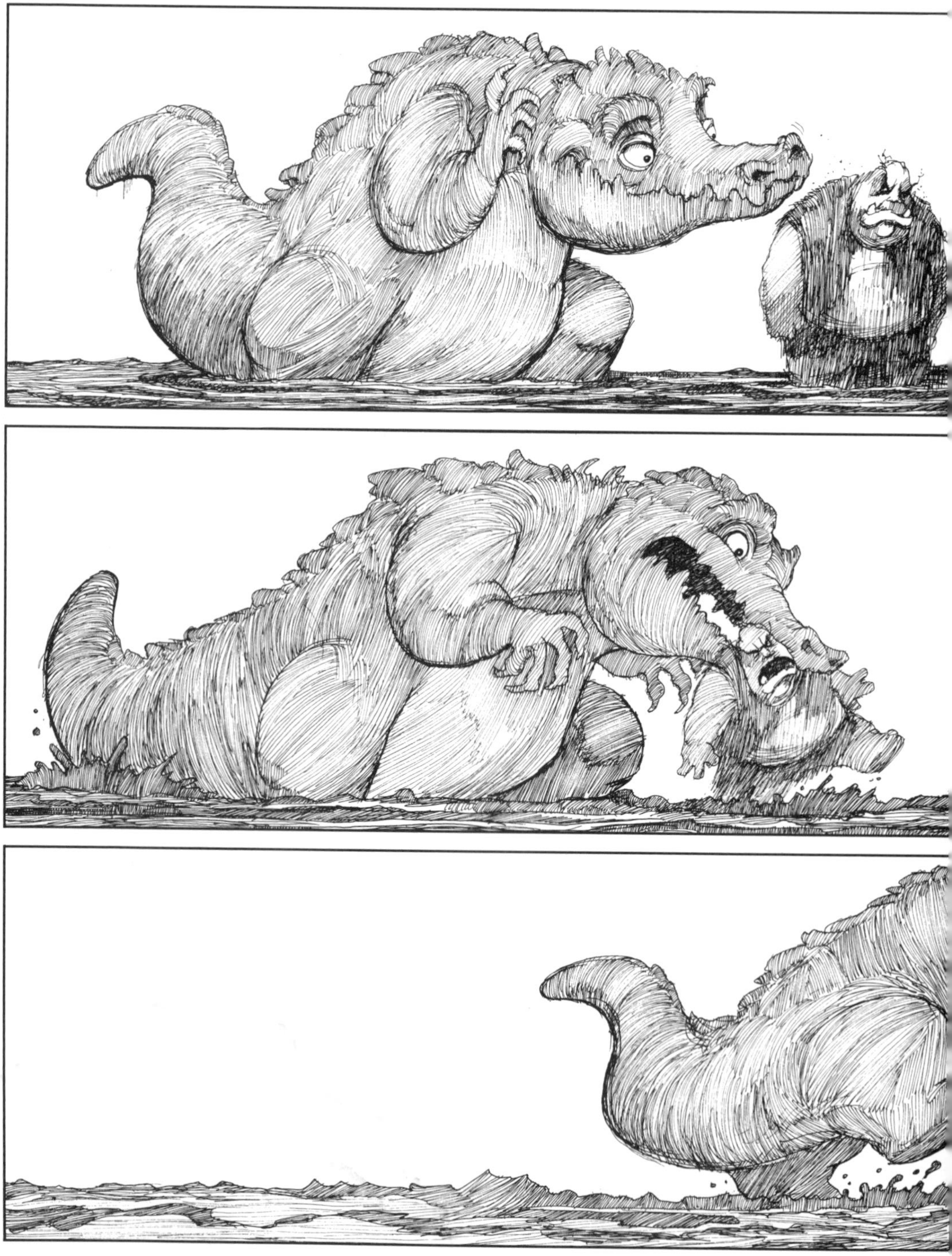

CHARACTERS

WART

SCROLLKEEPER AND HISTORIAN OF KORGI HOLLOW.

IVY

A YOUNG MOLLIE, WHO ALONG WITH HER KORGI CUB SPROUT, EMBARK ON ADVENTURES AROUND KORGI HOLLOW.

LUMP

A KIND CREATURE WHO WATCHES OVER KORGI HOLLOW.

SPROUT

THE YOUNG KORGI COMPANION OF IVY. HE HAS SPECIAL POWERS THAT HE IS JUST NOW DISCOVERING.

CREEPHOG

MYSTERIOUS CREATURES OF AN UNKNOWN ORIGIN WHO SPY ON IVY AND SPROUT.

MOLLIES

WOODLAND PEOPLE WHO INHABIT KORGI HOLLOW.

KORGIS

Loyal, fox-like creatures with big ears and large smiles, who live with the mollies in Korgi Hollow.

LIEUTENANT

A creature who keeps company with the Gallump.

GALLUMP MINIONS

Creatures who aid the Gallump and the Lieutenant.

A monster who lives beyond Korgi Hollow.

GALLUMP